LEGENDTOPIA
The Shadow Queen

LEGENDTOPIA

The Shadow Queen

Lee Bacon

Delacorte Press

Text copyright © 2017 by Lee Bacon
Jacket art copyright © 2017 by Alyssa Petersen

All rights reserved. Published in the United States by Delacorte Press, an imprint of Random House Children's Books, a division of Penguin Random House LLC, New York.

Delacorte Press is a registered trademark and the colophon is a trademark of Penguin Random House LLC.

randomhousekids.com

Educators and librarians, for a variety of teaching tools, visit us at RHTeachersLibrarians.com

Library of Congress Cataloging-in-Publication Data is available upon request.
ISBN 978-0-553-53406-1 (trade) — ISBN 978-0-553-53408-5 (ebook)

The text of this book is set in 13-point Jenson.
Interior design by Trish Parcell

Printed in the United States of America
10 9 8 7 6 5 4 3 2 1
First Edition

Random House Children's Books
supports the First Amendment and celebrates the right to read.

For Evan

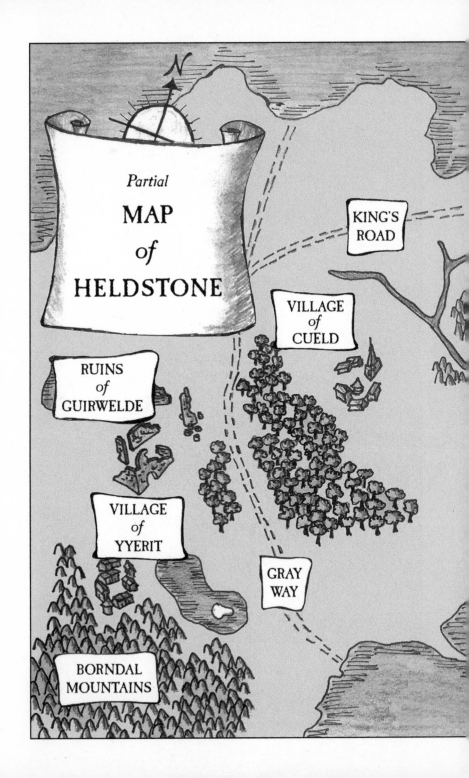

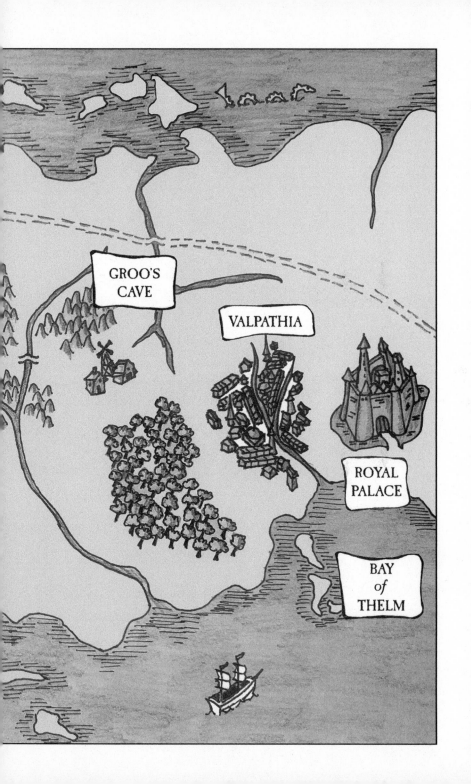

You are cordially invited to attend
The Luminary Ball
at the Royal Palace on the Night of Seven Moons
in honor of
King Frederick XIII and Queen Helena,
The Most Distinguished & Sovereign Rulers of Heldstone,
and
Prince Frederick XIV
His Royal Highness, Prince of the Realm.
Will you be attending?
YES   NO

RSVP to the Royal Palace via Fairy Courier
along with announcement of any additional guests
(which may include spouse, children, and distant
relatives, as well as maidservants, vassals, valets,
squires, stable boys, personal cooks, apprentices,
and others in your service).

Kara

Welcome to the worst day of my life.

Over the past twenty-four hours, I've been attacked by talking frogs, chased by a killer unicorn, and covered in dragon slobber. I found out my dad's being held prisoner in another dimension. I got into a fight with a couple of ogres in the boys' bathroom and watched an evil witch turn my normal little town into a fantasy theme park.

I'm Kara Estrada. Until recently, I was living a normal existence. Just a typical sixth grader at Shady Pines Middle School. But that all feels like a distant memory now. My world's been turned upside down, and I've been dumped headfirst into a fantasy story.

It all started with a field trip to Legendtopia (aka the cheesiest restaurant ever). I ended up getting separated from the rest of my class. Wandering into a walk-in refrigerator, I stumbled onto this strange miniature door.

And like an idiot, I opened it.

On the other side of the door, I found another world. A world known as Heldstone. That's where I first met Prince Fred. His full name is Prince Frederick Alexander Something Something Blah Blah Pointless Title Something Else the Fourteenth. But I just call him Prince Fred. It's a whole lot easier that way.

Anyway, the prince followed me back into my world. Unfortunately, so did the Sorceress. She worked her evil enchantment. She turned Legendtopia into a massive fortress. And she tried to transform Earth into her own dark kingdom.

We managed to stop the Sorceress. As her magical castle collapsed in flames all around us, we barely escaped.

Into the refrigerator and through the miniature door.

The magical portal to Fred's world.

Now that we're here, I'm one step closer to finding my dad again. He's being held captive somewhere in Heldstone.

And so here I am: stuck in this strange world, unsure whether I'll ever make it back home or see my dad again.

Like I said . . .

Worst. Day. Ever.

Prince Fred

What a marvelous day!

We defeated the Sorceress. We destroyed her castle. *And* we made it back through the miniature doorway. The portal to Heldstone. The portal to my world. And now we're about to embark on our very own epic quest to rescue Kara's father.

He discovered Heldstone the same way Kara did: by journeying through an enchanted refrigerator. But he never returned. For many years, Kara had no idea what happened to her father. Now she knows. He has been captive in my world all this time.

We're going to find him.

And we're going to bring him to safety.

I cast my gaze across the Chamber of Wizardry. This used to be the Sorceress's workshop. No telling what kind of vile magic still lurks here. Touch the wrong thing and you'll likely end up with a block of cheese for a hand.

The Sorceress is dead, I remind myself. *Vanquished in the fiery explosion that destroyed Legendtopia. Gone.*

So why do I have the eerie feeling that her presence still hangs in the air? Almost as if I'm being watched by her cruel black eyes.

"We should go." My voice cracks. "What I mean is—we shouldn't be seen here. In the Chamber of Wizardry. It will raise suspicions."

Kara nods. "This is your palace. Lead the way."

As we exit the Chamber of Wizardry, I cast one last glance across the room. And that's when something flickers at the edge of my vision. A dark shadow in the corner. But when I turn to get a better look, it's already gone.

———

We hurry down the hallway. Past the familiar sights of the palace: a porcelain vase of exotic flowers, a plush chair that nobody ever sits in, a portrait of my great-great-great-great-great-great-great-great-great-great-grandfather King Frederick the Bold.

Kara walks beside me, one hand clenched into a tight fist. She's holding an object of immense magical power and importance. An object we'll need if we want any chance of succeeding in our quest.

It's probably best if she doesn't lose it.

I catch a glimpse of our reflections in a gold-framed mirror. The two of us are a ghastly sight. The explosion in Legendtopia left its mark. Our faces are stained with ash. Our clothing is ripped and burned. We look like we just lost a wrestling match with a fire troll.

"In here. Quick."

I yank open a door and pull Kara into a servants' washroom. Fortunately, the small chamber is unoccupied.

Kara glances around, confused. "What are we doing in here?"

"Cleaning ourselves up." I shove a soapy cloth into Kara's hands. "Preferably *before* the washerwoman returns."

I grab a cloth of my own and begin scrubbing. Once I've cleaned the soot from my face and hair, I search the laundry piles until I find a suitable change of clothes for each of us.

"Here." I hold up a dress for Kara. "This looks your size."

A frown tugs at Kara's lips. "Isn't there something more . . . casual?"

"This isn't Urth. You can't go around dressed in a T-shirt and kreans—"

"They're called *jeans.*"

"The point is, you're a young lady. And in Heldstone, ladies wear dresses."

Kara sighs and grabs the dress. "Fine. Whatever."

I pull a curtain across the room to grant us privacy while we change. My new garments aren't as elegant as I'm accustomed to, but at least they don't look like they've been dragged through a furnace.

Once we're both dressed, I stuff our old attire into the bottom of a waste bin. Then I notice something hanging from a hook on the wall. A woman's purse. Its seams are sewn with gold silk. The front flap is studded with glittering jewels. These fine details are marred by a splatter of gravy on one edge. Which explains what such a costly purse is doing in a dingy room like this.

It's here to be cleaned.

I snatch the small purse off the rack and hold it out for Kara. "You should take this as well."

She eyes the accessory. "Looks expensive. Are you sure?"

"You can't keep carrying ... *that.*" I gesture to her clenched fist. To what we both know she's holding. "It's too important. What if you lose it? What if someone hears it in there?"

"All right. I get your point."

Kara carefully opens her hand. I catch my breath at the sight of what pops out. A small silver owl attached to a chain. Its wide silver eyes are blank, unseeing. But its wings beat the air. Up and down, up and down. Flying in a single direction.

Toward her father.

For years, Kara wore the owl as a necklace. She only just discovered that it's so much more than that.

It's a Chasing Charm. An object that has been enchanted to its Other. Kara's father gave it to her before he came to Heldstone. And now it's our guide. Our only way to find him.

Kara plucks the flying owl out of the air and gently inserts it into the purse. Closing the purse silences the tiny, flapping wings and keeps the necklace sealed inside.

"Here." I hand the purse to Kara. "Other than a little gravy stain, it's perfect. Just don't lose it."

Kara holds the purse close to her chest, almost as if she's holding her father. "No need to worry about that."

I nudge open the door to the washroom and we step outside. Just as the door clicks closed again, two gentlemen round the corner. One is exceedingly tall and thin, with white hair and the hunched posture of a question mark. The fellow beside him, on the other hand, resembles something more like a period. Small and round. His head is as spherical and smooth as a marble.

Even though I'm certain I've never met him, there's something oddly familiar about Question Mark. As soon as he catches my eye, I can tell he recognizes me. Not that this comes as a surprise. When you're the prince, everyone recognizes you.

"Ah, there you are!"

Question Mark's voice echoes down the hall as he strides in our direction. Period scrambles to keep up.

I lean close to Kara. "We mustn't let them know you're from Urth," I whisper. "Allow me to do the talking."

"Greetings, Prince Frederick." Question Mark speaks with a deep, authoritative voice. The type of voice that is accustomed to ordering servants and commanding armies. "It's a great honor to finally meet you in person."

"And you as well," I reply vaguely.

The period-shaped fellow beside him attempts a bow—not an easy task when you're as small and round as he is. "Humble greetings, Your Highness. My name is Gimothy Hudd. Chief Advisor to the Sturmenburg family."

Sturmenburg. As soon as I hear the name, I realize where I've seen Question Mark before. His portrait hangs in the

Hall of Diplomacy. Right between a pair of battle-axes and a mounted boar's head.

He's Grand Duke Nem Sturmenburg.

The Sturmenburgs are the second-wealthiest and second-noblest family in the kingdom. Their prestige is surpassed only by the monarchy. In other words, *my* family. The Sturmenburgs occupy the Southwest Province, a region known for its abundance of diamond mines. Which may explain why the grand duke's coat is clasped together by a most unusual variety of buttons.

Huge, gleaming diamonds.

An entire row of them.

His outfit alone is more valuable than a fleet of our navy's finest ships.

The grand duke arches an eyebrow. "I'm glad we found you. Your parents were ready to send out a search party."

Nerves twitch in my stomach. "A search party?"

"They said your servants found your room empty this morning," says Hudd. "And that you neglected to show up for tutoring."

I glance anxiously from the grand duke to his advisor. What am I supposed to tell them? I can't possibly admit the truth. That the reason I've been absent for the past twenty-four hours is because I traveled to another world, thwarted the Sorceress, and returned with an Urthling. They'll think I've lost my mind.

"Your Highness." The grand duke peers down at me. "I know precisely why you've gone missing."

My skin goes cold. "You do?"

"Of course I do. You've been busy preparing for the Luminary Ball."

The Luminary Ball. Of course. Every seven years, representatives from all corners of the kingdom journey to the Royal Palace to pledge their continued loyalty to the king and queen. For the entire week, the palace is stuffed with foreign visitors and their attendants. There are parades every day and feasts every night. It's glorious, magnificent, lavish. And it also makes a wonderful excuse.

"The Luminary Ball, that's correct." I let out a nervous chuckle. "Just thought I'd lend a hand. You know— greeting guests, ordering servants around. On a day such as this, every little bit helps."

"How very generous of you!" Hudd attempts to bow even lower—and nearly falls on his face. "Truly, you are the most benevolent and kindhearted boy in all of Heldstone!"

Kara rolls her eyes. Apparently, she's not as impressed by my greatness as Hudd.

"And might I inquire . . ." The grand duke turns his gaze in Kara's direction. "Who is your lovely friend?"

Before I can respond, Kara steps forward. "Hey, I'm Kara."

I wince. Here in Heldstone, "hay" is something the stable hand feeds to horses—*not* a word you use to greet visiting nobility.

Diamonds swim in the grand duke's eyes. The tiniest hint of a smile tugs at the corners of his thin mouth. "Quite a curious accent you have, Kara. Where are you from?"

Before Kara can make another blunder, I interject. "She's—uh . . . she's here for the Luminary Ball. Daughter of a visiting dignitary. They traveled here from . . ." I struggle to think of the farthest, most inaccessible backwoods of Heldstone. "From Stonk."

The grand duke tilts his head. "Stonk?"

"Precisely!"

"I toured through Stonk just last year. I don't recall meeting anyone with such an accent."

I grit my teeth. We've only just arrived, and already Kara's identity is coming into question. If anyone discovers that she's from Urth, even *I* won't be able to protect her. Scholars and wizards will travel from all corners of Heldstone to get a glimpse of the Urthling. She'll be locked away. Questioned endlessly. Poked and prodded. A scientific oddity. An alien. They'll never let her go.

The situation is bad enough already. And it's made even worse by what Kara says next.

"Prince Frederick's not telling the truth," she remarks. "I'm *not* from Stonk."

Kara

⁓

I don't like these guys.

The tall, hunched dude smiles down at me. But it's not a nice smile. It's a *secret* smile. Like he knows something I don't. And what about that bling? With all those diamonds, it's like he's wearing an entire jewelry store.

His buddy creeps me out even more. Short, round, and completely bald, Hudd has the beady pink eyes of a shaved rat.

"How dare you call the Royal Prince a liar!" His chins quiver with outrage. "Such statements cannot go unpunished! You ought to be hanged! Or beheaded. Or—"

"Now, Hudd." The grand duke places a steady hand on

his advisor's shoulder. His long fingers are ringed with too many diamonds to count. "We mustn't be too harsh on the girl. I'm sure she merely misspoke. Isn't that right, my dear?"

He raises one eyebrow. The secret smile never wavers.

I take a deep breath. Then I explain. "All I meant to say is, I didn't grow up in Stonk. I didn't grow up anywhere, really. Since my dad's a dignitary, he travels a lot. I went everywhere with him. That's why I have such a weird accent, I guess."

The grand duke's eyes move slowly from me to Prince Fred and back again. "See that, Hudd? The young lady has a perfectly convincing explanation. And you would've marched her off to the stocks without a second thought."

"My apologies," Hudd says, although he doesn't sound very apologetic.

Prince Fred clears his throat. "It's been a pleasure meeting you both. But we should really be on our way."

"Of course, Your Highness." The mysterious smile never leaves the grand duke's face. "I look forward to seeing you both this evening at the Luminary Ball."

A moment later, we're on the move again.

"That was a disaster," Prince Fred moans.

I glance in his direction. "What do you mean? I thought it went pretty well."

"You don't call the Royal Prince a liar! There are certain manners you must observe if you want to fit in here."

"I'm not here to *fit in.*" I give the sleeve of my dress a sharp tug. "I'm here to find my dad. Who cares what those two jerks think anyway? It's not like we're gonna be hanging around the palace very long. I say we leave right away. Get started searching for my dad."

"We can't leave yet."

"Why not?"

"Because," Fred replies, "we have a royal ball to attend."

My jaw drops. "My dad's life is at risk, and you want to go to . . . *a dance?*"

Fred's rapid footsteps click as he explains. "It's not just any dance. It's the Luminary Ball. The biggest event in the kingdom. Visitors from all across Heldstone come to pay their respects. Treaties are signed, alliances are renewed—"

"I don't care how big this stupid party is. We've got more important stuff to deal with."

Fred lets out a sigh. "I *have* to be there, Kara. I'm the prince. If I don't attend, the entire kingdom will know about it. My mother and father will send out an army to find me. We wouldn't make it past the city walls."

I search my brain for another option. A loophole. But I

never get the chance, because as we turn a corner we're met by a group of girls. Four of them, about our age. Dressed up in frilly gowns, with perfect hair and perfect makeup and perfect *everything*.

When they notice Prince Fred, the girls let out a chorus of gasps. It's like they've just spotted a celebrity. If this were my world, they'd probably start snapping selfies with the famous prince. But this isn't my world. And instead, the girls line up side by side in their poufy dresses, as if they've been practicing for just this moment.

The tallest and prettiest performs a curtsey. "Your Highness. What an absolute delight to see you again! It's been too long."

"Countess." The prince sweeps forward to kiss the girl's gloved hand. "How lovely that you could come!"

"I wouldn't miss it for the world."

The other three girls are quick to offer their own greetings. Each one curtseys a little lower than the last. This is followed by more hand-kissing from Prince Fred. By the time they're done smooching and complimenting each other, I'm about ready to barf.

The tallest girl glances in my direction. Her eyes match the enormous ring on her finger. Green and sparkling.

And sharp enough to draw blood.

"I don't believe we've met." Her crimson lips form an imitation of a smile. "My name is Francesca Gravuria Thomasina Ondietta te Xavienne, Countess of the Wrendstone Provinces. And who might you be?"

"Uh . . ." As I stare back at the girl, I suddenly feel very dull and very ordinary. My memory reaches back to what the prince said earlier. "My name's Kara Estrada. I'm visiting from Stonk."

The girl next to Francesca makes a face. "*Stonk?* I'm surprised you were able to travel all this way. I heard the entire population of Stonk has only a single healthy mule to share between them."

Two of the girls cover their mouths, trying to hide their laughter. But not Francesca. She silences her friends with a flick of her green eyes.

"I'm sure Stonk is a fascinating region," she says. "I've never been, of course. Father says it's too dangerous. Besides, the desert climates are terrible for my complexion."

One of her friends shakes her head vigorously. "Even the desolation of Stonk couldn't harm *your* complexion, Francesca!"

"I'd die to have your rosy glow," adds another.

But Francesca ignores her friends' brownnosing comments. All her attention is still trained on me. "Will you be attending the Luminary Ball, Kira?"

"It's *Kara*," I say. "And—uh . . . I'm not really sure I'll be able to—"

"Yes," Fred says. "She'll be there."

I shoot a glance in the prince's direction. With my eyes, I try to communicate that I have *zero* interest in attending some fancy ball. I've only been to one dance in my life. The Shady Pines Middle School Spring Splash. My best friend, Marcy, and I spent the entire night standing awkwardly in the corner, trying not to spill punch on our dresses.

The worst part was the worrying. *What if I'm a terrible dancer? How will I know where to put my hands? Am I going to step on some poor guy's toes?* As the night stretched on, though, I got something *new* to worry about. *Why haven't any boys asked me to dance? Am I putting off a dork vibe? Is all this nervous sweating making my armpits stink?*

So, yeah . . . dances aren't really my thing.

I'm not the only one disappointed that I'll be attending the Luminary Ball. By the way Francesca and her friends are glaring at me, I know they don't want me there, either.

But when Prince Fred looks at the group of girls, their expressions instantly transform. Their lips stretch into tight smiles. Their delicate hands clasp with mock excitement. Their voices chirp like exotic birds.

"How marvelous!"

"Such a thrill!"

"I'm sure it shall be far better than anything you could ever experience in *Stonk*."

Francesca narrows her sparkling green eyes. "You simply *must* come with us. We're on our way to the Grand Drawing Room."

"Oh, no thanks," I say quickly.

"I'm afraid it isn't optional. All the young ladies will be there. We're getting ready for the ball!"

"That's okay. Really. I actually need to—"

Francesca grabs my wrist. Her fingernails dig into my skin, but she's beaming at me like we're BFFs. "I truly *must* insist. Now come along, Kira. We shall have ever so much fun!"

I toss a desperate look at Prince Fred, but he only manages a sympathetic shrug and mouths the words, *I'm sorry.*

Francesca yanks my wrist. Her friends loop arms around my waist. The group surrounds me, guiding me away from the only person I know in this world.

Prince Fred

As Kara vanishes around the corner, my fingers twist into a tense knot. She's only just arrived in Heldstone, and already I'm letting her out of my sight.

But she's in good hands. I've known Francesca my entire life. The bond between our families stretches back hundreds of years. Our parents have even talked about a possible marriage.

Not that I have any interest in such a thing. I've told Mother and Father countless times that I refuse to consider *any* kind of arranged wedding. I don't care about "strategic alliances" (Father's words) or "family obligations" (Mother's favorite excuse). A marriage shouldn't be forced onto a person like a tutoring assignment.

I'm sure Francesca feels exactly the same way.

And that she'll treat Kara wonderfully.

—

When I return to my bedchamber, I'm met by a half-dozen servants. Standing at attention, hands clasped behind their backs, ready to do anything and everything I ask of them. It's a familiar sight. From the moment I was born, I've been surrounded by servants. Men and women devoted to one—and only one—thing:

Me.

"Greetings, Your Highness," says the head servant. "We laid out your attire for the Luminary Ball."

"Would you like us to help you try it on?" says another.

"Or perhaps you'd prefer that we draw you a bath first?"

I glance across the row of servants. Crisp uniforms, stiff postures. Waiting for my command.

I begin to give an order but stop myself. Instead, I clear my throat. And when the words come, they aren't what I expected. "Actually, I won't be needing your help. I've decided to get dressed on my own today."

A flicker of surprise flashes across the servants' faces.

"Pardon me, Your Highness," says one. "I may have misunderstood. It sounded as though you said . . . that you—"

"Want to get dressed on my own." I nod. "You heard me correctly."

The servants look baffled. And I understand why. All these years, I've come to rely on them for everything. They ensure that I'm well dressed, well groomed, and well fed. Protected inside a bubble of comfort and convenience. Safe and secure . . .

And unable to do a thing for myself.

All that changed once I entered Kara's world. During my time on Urth, there weren't any servants to comb my hair or fluff my pillows. It was often difficult. But I also experienced something I'd never encountered before: independence. For the first time, I was in control of my own life. And I rather liked the feeling.

"In fact," I add, "I won't be needing your assistance for the rest of the day."

The servants cast confused glances at one another. They've rigorously trained for a million different situations and scenarios. Obviously, this isn't one of them.

After a long moment of silence, the head servant manages to speak. "But, Your Highness? Who will fasten your boots? And clean your nails? And pluck your eyebrows?"

"I will." I straighten my shoulders, feeling more

independent already. "Or—at least I shall try. That's the only way to learn, right?"

"But—"

"That will be all," I interrupt. "You may go now."

The servants linger for a moment longer, as if afraid this is all some elaborate trick. But they're required to obey my orders. Even the ones they don't understand. And eventually, they file out of the room, leaving me alone.

Or . . . *almost* alone.

A small, furry shape emerges from behind a dresser and slinks in my direction. I can hear its purring, even from the other end of the bedchamber.

"Hello, Xyler," I say to the cat. "How long have you been here?"

"Long enough," he replies mysteriously.

All the other cats that inhabit the palace spend their time lurking around the kitchen, hoping to gobble up any morsels of food that might fall to the floor. But not Xyler. He can usually be found in the Royal Tutor's chambers. And while I can barely keep myself awake during my daily lessons, Xyler often curls up on the nearest bookshelf, his ears pricked attentively to the tutor's words.

Xyler's tail weaves behind him, but his eyes are steady. They shine up at me like two shimmering moons. "Pray tell, Your Highness . . . how was Urth?"

I stare at the cat for a long moment, certain I must've misheard him. "What did you just say?"

"Urth . . . how was it?"

Kara and I told nobody of our voyage to her world. "I . . . I have no idea what you're talking about."

One look into Xyler's hazel eyes and I know he isn't falling for my deception.

"Worry not," he says. "I won't tell anyone. Cats are extremely skilled when it comes to keeping secrets."

"What makes you think I've been to Urth?"

"Well, for one thing, you didn't come to your room last night."

"Perhaps I slept in a different room. This palace has plenty of them."

"That's what I originally thought. But as soon as you walked through the door, I knew there was another explanation. You journeyed to Urth."

"How . . . ?" The words catch in my throat. "How could you possibly know?"

Licking his paw, the cat explains. "You humans always underestimate the sense of smell. Even from here I'm able to detect several distinct scents on you. There's soapy laundry. That must explain why you're wearing such unusual garments. You took them from a servants' washroom."

The cat takes a step closer, sniffing the air.

"There's also a strong odor of smoke and flames," he says. "You must've been caught in a fire."

My memory tumbles back to Legendtopia. Flames engulfing the Sorceress's fortress. Staggering through curtains of smoke and ash.

Xyler's unblinking gaze hangs on me. "And then there's another scent. Buried under the smells of soapy laundry and flames. The faint whiff of Urth."

"How do you know what Urth smells like?"

"Because." The cat's tail flicks. "I've smelled it once before."

⌒

Three years ago, Xyler was napping under a sofa when an oddly dressed man came stumbling into the hallway, looking lost.

"Greetings, strange traveler," said the cat. "May I offer any assistance?"

The man's only response was to stare at Xyler in utter astonishment.

The cat tilted his head. "I apologize if I've offended you—"

"It's not that." The man ran a hand through his dark hair. "It's just—cats don't talk where I come from."

"And where might *that* be?"

The man considered this question for a second. "A place called Urth," he finally said.

"Urth." It was the first time Xyler would hear the peculiar word. But it certainly wouldn't be the last. Over the next three years, everyone in Heldstone would become captivated by the legend of Urth. A place where lights ignite with the flip of a switch. Where all the knowledge in the world can fit into the palm of your hand. Where people travel in horseless carriages and machines soar through the skies.

But on that day, the first day that Xyler met the strange traveler, Urth was completely new.

Xyler helped the man find his way out of the palace without encountering any guards. When they reached the back tunnels, the cat paused in the doorway.

"This is as far as I can go," he said. "I wish you good fortune in your travels."

"Thank you," said the man.

"One last question before you depart."

"Of course."

"What is your name?"

The man glanced deep into the tunnel that led beyond the walls of the palace. Into a new world. Heldstone.

Then he turned back to the cat. "My name is Santiago Estrada."

—

By the time Xyler is done with the tale, I have to steady myself against the wall.

"This is incredible." I shake my head, staring at the cat. "Why didn't you say something sooner?"

"I told you already," Xyler replies. "Cats are excellent at keeping secrets."

Preparations for the Luminary Ball can wait. Kara needs to know about this. Now. If only we possessed the technology of Urth, I would call her on a Self-Own. All Urthlings seem to carry the sleek devices in their pockets, allowing them to speak and write to each other, no matter how far apart they may be. But this isn't Urth. And if I want to talk to Kara, I'll have to speak with her in person.

"You must do something for me," I say to Xyler.

The cat stands at attention. "Of course, Your Highness."

"I need you to find someone."

"Whom shall I find?"

I take a deep breath. "Her name is Kara. And she's the daughter of Santiago Estrada."

I begin to describe Kara to Xyler, but he stops me with a raised paw.

"I presume she smells like you, right?" says the cat. "A mixture of soap, fire, and Urth."

I nod. "You should be able to find her in the Grand Drawing Room. She set off in that direction a little while ago with Countess Francesca—"

"Your fiancée?"

"Francesca's not my *fiancée!*" My tone sounds more defensive than I'd intended. Lowering my voice, I add, "Our parents have discussed the topic, but I can assure you— neither of us has the slightest interest in an arranged marriage."

The cat looks skeptical. "If you say so."

Kara

Ugh. These girls are the *worst*.

Francesca and her friends guide me through the palace in a tight bundle of giggling and teasing. If you saw us from a distance, you'd think they actually like me. But if you look closer, you might notice Francesca's fingernails digging into my arm. Or her friends "accidentally" jabbing me with their elbows every time we turn a corner. Or the way all their compliments are actually insults.

"I love your dress! It's so simple and cheap."

"And your hair! It must've taken hours to make it look so authentically messy."

"How refreshing to meet someone who doesn't care about her appearance!"

Heldstone might be a different dimension, but I've come across girls like this before. Pretty and popular . . . and completely spoiled. They strut through the world like it's their own personal red carpet. Back at Shady Pines Middle School, kids show off their status with expensive clothes and new phones. Apparently, here they brag about all the servants they employ and how many castles they'll inherit.

I would ditch them, but where am I supposed to go? This palace is a vast maze of twisting hallways and ornate rooms. I might never find Prince Fred again.

Looks like I'm stuck with Francesca and her groupies.

We push through a doorway (another elbow jabs me in the side) and begin making our way up a winding stairway.

Up and up and up.

"Uh . . . where did you say we were going again?" I ask.

Francesca's grasp on my arm tightens. "You'll find out soon enough, Kira."

I swallow the urge to correct her. It doesn't matter anyway. No matter how many times I've told them my name's *Kara*, they keep saying it wrong.

At the top of the stairs, Francesca opens a steel door. For

a second, everything goes white. A blinding light smacks me in the face. Unable to see anything, I stagger through the doorway with the rest of the group.

When my vision finally clears, I take in my new surroundings. We're outside, standing on some kind of balcony. Looking past the thick stone railing, I feel my legs melt away beneath me. The view is beyond belief. Up to this point, all I've seen of Prince Fred's world is the palace. And don't get me wrong. It's impressive. But now that I'm outside, the spectacular scale of Heldstone unfolds in front of me.

An immense city stretches out past the palace walls. Sunlight glistens across tall golden spires. Wooden houses with thatch roofs lean crookedly over cobblestoned streets and bustling markets. The air fills with the faint sounds of clopping hooves and clattering carriage wheels. If I squint, I can just barely read the painted wooden signs on shops far below.

The city's population bustles through the streets, humans interacting with the kinds of residents who look like they just wandered off the set of a megabudget fantasy movie. Squat, hairy figures with bulbous noses and jutting chins (dwarfs, I'm guessing). Tall, elegant men and women with luminescent skin (elves, most likely). A hulking gray dude that must be an ogre. The monster grunts as it drags a cart behind it.

Looming in the distance is a vast mountain range. A winged creature appears from behind one of the snow-capped peaks. At first I assume it's a bird. But this thing's way too big. Besides, birds don't have long, spiky tails. And they definitely don't breathe puffs of flame from their nostrils.

My heart skips a few beats when I realize ... it's a dragon.

There's so much more to take in. But my attention is snapped away from the incredible scenery by a sudden realization. The balcony has only one exit: the door we just walked through.

I turn to the group. "I thought we were going to get ready for the ball?"

Francesca's nasty gaze narrows on me. "*You're* not going to the ball."

"What're you talking about?" I take a step toward the door, but Francesca's groupies block the way. "Why are you doing this?"

"Because." Francesca flits a strand of her perfect hair out of her perfect face. "I don't appreciate some backwater nobody attempting to move in on my fiancé."

I tilt my head. Now I'm really confused. "Your *fiancé?*"

"Prince Frederick," Francesca snaps. "We're going to be married someday."

"Married? But you're only kids!"

Francesca lets out a very unladylike snort. "You can't possibly be *that* stupid? Even a nobody from Stonk must surely be aware that my family has a strategic connection to Prince Frederick's family. It makes perfect sense to solidify that alliance with a marriage."

I retrace Francesca's words in my mind. "Strategic." "Alliance." "But that's no reason to get married—"

"Just cut the Little Miss Innocent act already!" Francesca jabs a manicured finger in my face. "We both know that a coalition with my family is the only way Prince Frederick will hold on to the crown. Especially now, with Grand Duke Sturmenburg consolidating power. He wants the throne. The only way that Prince Frederick can hold power is by marrying me, by making me his queen."

My brain feels like it's buffering, trying to keep up with Francesca's claims. *Grand Duke Sturmenburg.* That was the tall, hunched guy we met earlier. The one sporting all the diamonds. He's planning a takeover?

Everything's moving too quickly. Francesca's already talking again.

"So don't get any ideas about stealing the prince away from me," she snaps.

I shake my head. "I'm not trying to steal *anyone.*"

"She's lying," spits one of the groupies.

Francesca's friends stalk forward. They might have the dainty bodies of ballerinas, but they're staring me down like wrestlers before a cage match. The nearest girl forces me backward until my spine is pressed against the stone railing of the balcony.

I peek over the edge and instantly regret it. It's a looooong way down.

"Wouldn't want to accidentally fall," one of the groupies purrs. "From this far up, you'd leave quite a mess for the servants to clean. Not that anyone else would mind. After all, you're just a little nobody from Stonk."

A gust of wind blows my hair into my eyes, but I'm too nervous about letting go of the railing to brush it away. "Y-you can't do this."

"Actually, you're mistaken." An arrogant smile appears on Francesca's face. "We can do whatever we want. Leave my fiancé alone. Or else next time, we won't be so polite." She gestures to her groupies. "Let's go. I'm sure Kira would like a little time alone to think."

The girls spin and make their exit. The metal door slams shut behind them.

As soon as I'm alone, my entire body dissolves into a fit of shivering. The mean girls at Shady Pines Middle School are nothing compared to Francesca and her friends. I don't care what she said; I need to talk to the prince. To tell him about the Grand Duke Sturmenburg. But when I try to open the door, it won't budge. I rattle the handle. Still nothing.

I'm locked out.

Prince Fred

—

By the time I reach the Royal Ballroom, the place is crammed with dignitaries from every corner of Heldstone. Visiting nobles, elven ambassadors, representatives from the Intercontinental Wizards Guild. All of them dressed in their finest attire. Servants weave between guests, carrying food and drinks on silver platters. Children giggle and point at the jesters on stilts who lurch like giants throughout the room. Dancers twirl across the floor, accompanied by music from a sixty-piece orchestra. Glowing fairies drift through the air like twinkling, pinwheeling stars.

But no sign of Kara.

I scan the crowd, hoping for a glimpse of her face. She's nowhere to be found. She must still be in the Grand Drawing Room. Most likely, Countess Francesca and her friends are taking extra time to prepare for the ball.

What other explanation could there be?

My eyes are drawn to an elegant couple near the center of the room. The tall man with eyes the color of the sky on a clear summer day. And the woman with long golden hair. Each wears a sparkling crown of jewels and gold.

My mother and father. King and Queen of Heldstone.

As I make my way toward them, the crowd parts like a wave. Reverent whispers, respectful bows. When Mother spots me, her face breaks into a relieved smile.

"My dearest son! At last, you're here." She clasps me in a hug. Then she eyes me more closely. "Is it true?"

My stomach twists. "Is *what* true?"

"That you've been busy helping in the preparations?"

"Ah, of course." My eyes drop to the floor. That's better than lying to my parents' faces. "I've been *quite* busy with the preparations."

"I'm proud of you, Frederick." Father runs a hand through my hair. "A true ruler puts the interests of the kingdom before his own. With all the commotion here in the palace, you stepped forward to help."

Mother's delighted gaze shines down on me. "You'll make a wonderful king someday!"

I wish I could tell them about the quest I'm about to embark on. But they'd never allow me to venture out of the palace on such a risky mission. Not in a million years.

And so instead of admitting the truth, I wrap my arms around Father. "Thank you for showing me how to be a real king."

Next I hug Mother. "I love you. I always will."

"We love you, too, Frederick." Mother gives me a closer look. "Are you all right?"

"Of course." My eyes drop to the floor. "I just wanted to let you know how I feel."

In case I never get another chance.

"That's very nice of you, son." Father pats me on the shoulder. The lights of twirling fairies glisten across the rings on his fingers. "Now get out there and enjoy the ball before it's over!"

I take a deep breath and do as he instructs. But before my parents are swallowed by the crowd, I wave back at them one last time.

I just hope it's not the last time I ever see them.

Kara

⌒

As the sun vanishes behind the tall mountains, an extraordinary sight appears in the darkening sky. There isn't just a single moon. There are *seven* of them. Pale silver spheres floating in space. A couple of them are enormous. Others are much smaller than the moon you see from my world.

For a few seconds, all I can do is stand there and stare out at the foreign sky. Then reality comes crashing back into my life.

Hours have gone by.

And I'm still here.

Abandoned by Francesca and her evil entourage.

Stuck on the balcony.

I've tried pounding on the metal door, but nobody ever responds. I've looked out over the railing, waving my arms and screaming at the top of my lungs, but the people far below don't notice. Everyone else is way too busy with the ball.

The ball I'm supposed to be attending.

It's not like I care about missing some stupid dance. It's what comes after the stupid dance that I'm more interested in. That's when Prince Fred and I are setting out to find my dad.

But not if I'm stuck on this balcony.

I need to figure out a way inside the palace. The question is . . . *how?* Glancing to my right, I feel my stomach plummet. There's nothing out there but an ugly gargoyle and a two-hundred-foot drop. In the other direction, a narrow ledge runs along the stone wall, leading to another balcony. It looks like the balcony I'm standing on. Except for *one* difference.

On the other balcony, the door is wide open.

It might be my only way back inside. But getting there won't be easy. The ledge is very narrow. One false step could result in a deadly fall.

I back away from the railing. I can't do it. I'm too afraid.

My gaze lands on the purse. It's been clenched in my hand ever since Fred and I left the laundry room. Opening it just enough to reach inside, I grasp the necklace.

The little silver owl immediately bursts into the air. But it doesn't get far. Not while I'm holding its chain like a leash. The light of seven moons traces its features. The bird's wings flap persistently. Its beak points toward the mountain ranges in the distance.

Dad gave me the necklace three years ago, the day before he disappeared from my life. All this time, I've kept it close. A reminder of him. Of the way he smiled when he gave it to me. Of the words he spoke. *If you keep this necklace with you*, he said, *it'll bring you closer to me*.

At the time, I had no idea what he was *really* trying to tell me. Now I do. The silver owl necklace is a Chasing Charm. Which basically means it's a magical GPS navigator. With only one objective.

To make its way back to my dad.

I cautiously return the necklace to the purse. One glimpse at the owl was enough to wash away the uncertainty. I knew this journey was going to be tough. And there's a good chance it's just going to get a lot tougher. But none of that can stop me.

I'm going to find my dad.

I'm going to rescue him.

And I'm going to bring him back home.

Clenching my jaw with determination, I step forward again. Fear swims inside my head, but instead of focusing on it, I train my concentration on the task in front of me. Swinging both legs over the railing, I carefully step onto the ledge. My back is pressed against the chilly stone wall. The tips of my feet stick out over the edge.

I shuffle sideways a step. Then another. Then—

A gust of wind barrels past. My hair flails everywhere. The bottom of my dress billows outward. And in my panic, I do the worst thing you can possibly do in a moment like this.

I look down.

A dizzying wave of terror sweeps across my entire body. My heartbeat thunders in my eardrums.

Deep breath. *You've got this, Kara.* The voice in my head is nearly lost in the rush of wind, but it's enough.

Careful to keep from looking down again, I swing my focus back to the balcony. The open door. I start moving toward it again. One tiny, shuffling step after another. Wind whips all around me, but I keep moving. A little at a time. The balcony gets closer. And closer. And—

Next thing I know, my arms are hugging the railing like

it's my best friend. I lift myself over the stone barrier and my feet come to rest on the balcony floor.

I made it.

As I approach the open door, I hear a pair of voices. They're coming from inside. Creeping forward as quietly as possible, I peek through the doorway. Standing in the center of the room are the two men I met hours earlier. Grand Duke Sturmenburg and his advisor, Gimothy Hudd.

"We've come so far," says the grand duke. "We can't give up now. Not when we're so close."

His hunched posture looms crookedly over the advisor's short, round frame. A crackling fireplace sends its flickering light across the room. Shadows jump and dance, gathering in the corners.

"You deserve the crown," replies Hudd. "You have the resources. You have the army—"

"It doesn't matter how many diamonds we amass, or how many troops," the grand duke growls. "The people are loyal to the king and queen. And their spoiled little son."

"Then we abide by our original plan," replies Hudd. "We kill them. And Prince Frederick."

I inhale a sharp breath. Luckily, the wind on the balcony is too loud for anyone inside to hear. From the first moment I met these guys, I didn't like them. But I had no idea just how terrible they truly are.

"We can't kill them, you fool," the grand duke snaps. "Not without *her*. Only she possesses enough dark power to sway the people."

"Does anyone know what happened to her?"

The grand duke shakes his head. "Only that she hasn't been seen since yesterday."

"How can the Sorceress disappear at a time like this? I thought we had an agreement."

A movement at the edge of the room pulls my attention away from the men. A shadow slides across the wall. At first, I don't trust what I've just witnessed. It's impossible. Must be a trick of the light. The blazing fireplace has a way of making you see things.

But then the shadow moves again. And this time, I'm sure . . . this isn't just my imagination. This is real.

The dark shape drips down to the floor and shifts toward the two men. Soon it's beside them. And I'm not the only one who's noticed it, either. Sturmenburg and Hudd have gone silent. The two of them stare, wide-eyed, at the shadow near their feet.

Hudd points a chubby trembling finger. "Wh-what . . . is . . . that?"

The grand duke can only shake his head. All the color

drains from his face as the shadow begins to rise. A human form ascending from the pool of darkness. The figure has no face, no features. Only darkness.

A living shadow.

Fear claws at my heart. The Sorceress is still alive.

My memory tumbles back to Legendtopia. Everything was engulfed in fire and smoke. And through the chaos I spotted the Sorceress. As the destruction closed in on her, she spread her arms. Her eyes closed and her lips moved. As if whispering a spell. And suddenly, she was gone. Replaced by a shadow of herself. A shadow that looked exactly like what I'm seeing now.

I'd hoped it was an illusion. A trick of the fire and smoke. But now I know—it was real. The Sorceress didn't die in Legendtopia. She transformed herself into a shadow, escaped with us through the miniature doorway . . .

And now she's here in Heldstone.

She's looming right before my eyes.

The shadow turns its dark head from Hudd to Sturmenburg. When it speaks, the voice seems to be nowhere and everywhere at once. Echoing through the room and whispering into my ear. The only thing I know for sure is . . . the voice belongs to the Sorceress.

"You speak of me as though I'm not here," she says.

Sturmenburg stares at the dark shape with fear and awe. "Sorceress. What happened?"

"That doesn't concern you." Her voice hangs heavy in the air. "All you need to know is that I have taken a new form. And though I may lack a body, my powers have grown beyond belief."

Hudd's eyes narrow. "How can we be certain it's really you? What if this is some trick?"

In a heartbeat, the shadow sweeps toward Hudd. The dark shape crackles with unseen power. I can feel it from across the room, like a storm cloud about to burst.

"I do not play *tricks*," the Sorceress growls. "And if you doubt me again, I will make you pay."

"Pardon my advisor's idiocy." The grand duke does his best to act like his usual arrogant self, but I can hear the dread behind his words. "It's just . . . your appearance is . . . not what we expected."

"Appearance matters not. My current form may have changed, but my intentions haven't. We must kill the king and queen." The shadow clenches its dark hands with fury. "*And* Prince Frederick."

"How do you propose we do that?" Sturmenburg asks.

"With Malinwrought."

The grand duke and his advisor exchange a glance. It's

obvious they know as much about this Malin-whatever stuff as I do. Nothing.

"Malinwrought is a poison. Colorless, odorless," the Sorceress says. "And completely untraceable. One sip causes the victim to become ill. But not all at once. Like most illnesses, it begins slowly. Steadily worsening. Until eventually, the victim falls into a sleep from which there is no waking. Anyone who drinks it will be dead in three days."

Hudd shakes his head. "If this poison is so effective, why have I never heard of it?"

"Because all traces of Malinwrought vanished from Heldstone five centuries ago."

"Well, that's just wonderful!" Hudd throws up his hands in frustration. "We're taking orders from a *shadow*. Who commands us to kill the Royal Family. With a poison that doesn't exist."

"Hudd, watch your tongue," the grand duke warns.

But the advisor isn't done complaining yet. "We had a plan! We were supposed to meet here at the appointed time with the Sorceress! But look who shows up instead! A ghoulish monstrosity! This is an insult, and I won't stand for it any—"

Hudd's words choke to a halt when the Sorceress

presses her shadow finger against his forehead. Eyes bulging, his hands clasp his throat as he drops to his knees.

"I told you already." The Sorceress's dark finger never leaves Hudd's forehead. "If you doubt me again, I will make you pay."

The advisor tries to reply, but the only sound he can make is a weak gurgle. His round face goes from blue to purple. With a final gasp, he falls face-first onto the floor.

He doesn't move again.

The shadow turns its faceless face toward the grand duke. When the Sorceress begins speaking again, it's as if nothing's happened. As if there *isn't* a dead guy lying at her dark feet.

"As I was saying, Malinwrought disappeared from the world five hundred years ago. That is the common belief, at least. However, there remains one last vial. Preserved all this time. I have it hidden in the Chamber of Wizardry. It's more than enough to eliminate the Royal Family."

The shadow takes a silent step toward Sturmenburg.

"I will show you where to find the Malinwrought," says the Sorceress. "And you will put it into the drinks of the king, queen, and prince. Is that understood?"

The grand duke's unsteady gaze hangs on Hudd's body for a long moment. Then he nods.

"Excellent. As the poison does its work, I will use my enchantment to ensure that fate follows a suitable path. The Royal Family will die. Everyone will assume it was illness. You will be named their successor. And together we will rule the kingdom."

As the Sorceress describes her plan, the fear slowly fades from the grand duke's face. He's no longer staring at the dead man on the floor. Instead, his eyes are trained on the shadow in front of him. A faint grin tugs at his lips.

"At last," he whispers. "I will have the power I deserve."

"*We*," corrects the Sorceress in a stern voice. "*We* will have the power *we* deserve."

The grand duke nods quickly. His expression is a mix of terror and awe and ambition. "Of course. *We*. Without a doubt."

The shadow crosses the room in the blink of an eye. A flicker of darkness that flows across the rug and returns to a human shape in the doorway.

"Now come along," she says. "We have work to do."

Prince Fred

—

Where in the seven moons is Kara?

I continue searching the crowded dance floor, the rows of tables, the marble balconies overlooking the ballroom. Still no sign of her. I'm on my way to the main doors when I'm suddenly met by Francesca.

As I observe her glowing smile, her luxurious gown, her perfect hair, I'm strangely reminded of something I encountered in Kara's world. A television. A device that flashes and sparkles with such remarkable radiance that you can barely look away. And yet, when you glance behind the screen, there's only emptiness.

A breathtaking surface, with nothing behind it. That's what I see when I look at Francesca.

"Your Highness!" Francesca dips into a curtsey. "You look spectacular this evening."

"As do you, Countess," I reply quickly. "Do you . . . uh—happen to know where Kara is?"

Francesca's head tilts. "Who?"

"Kara. You accompanied her to the Grand Drawing Room earlier. To get ready for the ball."

"Oh, the girl from Stonk!"

"Precisely. She was supposed to be here, but I can't seem to find her."

"Really? How odd." Francesca takes a sip from her silver goblet. "She came with us to the drawing room. But when we left for the ball, she stayed behind. Said she wanted to make sure her gown was absolutely perfect."

"*Kara* said that?"

Francesca nods. "Perhaps she got lost trying to find her way. The palace hallways can be confusing. Especially for someone so far outside her natural element."

I can imagine Kara getting lost in the palace. But spending extra time getting fitted for a ball gown? Highly unlikely. Not that Francesca seems concerned. She glides closer to me. Her slender hand grazes my arm.

"It's very noble of you to devote such attention to one plain little girl," she whispers into my ear. "But you mustn't let it ruin your night. After all, *you* are the Royal Prince. The Luminary Ball is in honor of *your* family. You should socialize, enjoy yourself, dance."

Francesca's fingers slide down my arm and take hold of my hand.

"And speaking of dancing—"

Before she can continue, a new voice joins our conversation.

"The two of you make an enchanting couple."

Grand Duke Sturmenburg looms over us. His long fingers are decorated with more diamonds than I can count. In each hand, he holds a goblet. One gold, one silver.

I start to tell Sturmenburg that Francesca and I aren't a couple, but her response comes quicker.

"Thank you!" she chirps.

"This Luminary Ball is a most magnificent occasion." The grand duke takes a moment to admire the vast room, the joyous crowds. Then his gaze returns to us. "There is only one thing missing."

"And what might that be?" I ask.

"Isn't it obvious?" A smile pulls at his thin lips. "You have nothing to drink, Your Highness."

"Why, goodness! He's right!" Judging by the look on

Francesca's face, you'd think I was missing a finger, not a drink. "Allow me to fetch a servant at once!"

"That won't be necessary," the grand duke says. "I happen to have an extra cup of sparkling honeydrop."

He bends forward, extending the golden goblet.

I wave away the offer. "Many thanks, but I was actually looking for—"

"Surely it can wait." The grand duke's voice is friendly but insistent. "At least long enough for a toast."

"Wonderful idea!" Francesca raises her own goblet. "What shall we toast to?"

"To the Royal Family," the grand duke suggests. "May your reign last another thousand years."

Francesca's goblet rises higher. "To the Royal Family!"

The two of them are staring at me with expectant smiles. The goblet presses closer to me. Golden liquid swirls inside the golden cup. If a toast is what it takes to get me out of this conversation, then so be it.

With a sigh, I grab the cup. As it leaves the grand duke's long fingers, a strange fire blazes behind his pale eyes. A jumbled blur of music and festivities surrounds us, but his gaze never leaves me. Waiting, watching.

"Cheers."

I raise the goblet and press it to my lips.

Kara

I'm running as fast as I can. I just don't know if it's fast enough. It doesn't help that I have no idea where I'm going. This palace is an enormous labyrinth of fancy hallways. The Luminary Ball must be going on around here somewhere, but it's not like I can search for it on Google Maps.

With each footstep, my memory cycles through a twisted playlist of the encounter I just witnessed. The shadow rising, becoming the Sorceress. Hudd's gruesome death. And that strange, foreign word. *Malinwrought*. An untraceable poison. Anyone who drinks it will be dead within three days.

The grand duke plans to slip the poison into the drinks of Prince Fred and his parents.

I have to get to them before that happens. I have to warn them.

But first, I have to *find* them.

At the top of a stairway, I come across a guard leaning on his spear.

"Excuse me, sir." I pause, huffing to catch my breath. "Do you know where the Luminary Ball is?"

The guard's forehead wrinkles as he examines me. His eyes narrow at my simple dress. My scuffed knees. My ash-stained slippers.

"How'd you get up here?" he asks.

"I . . . I was invited. By Prince Fred."

"You mean Prince *Frederick?* His Royal Highness?"

I wince at my own mistake. But there's no backing down now. "Of course, yeah. I mean—yes, sir."

The guard's grip on his spear tightens. "The commander warned us to be on high alert for any commoners trying to sneak into the Luminary Ball. I don't know how you got all the way up here, but you won't be going anywhere *near* the Royal Family."

The guard stalks toward me. The shaft of his spear clangs against the floor with every step. But then he freezes at the sound of a voice.

"Please step aside, guard. Can't you see the girl's late enough as it is?"

I whirl sideways, but nobody's there. Then my gaze drops to the floor. And that's when I see the cat. Gray and black fur, white paws, and wide hazel eyes peering up at me.

If the guard is surprised by the talking cat, he does a good job of hiding it.

"Xyler?" he says. "You know this girl?"

The cat nods. And when he opens his mouth, he speaks in a crisp, formal voice. "Indeed I do. She's a personal guest of the prince. And I doubt he would approve of your intimidating her."

I don't know what's weirder. That I'm witnessing a conversation between a palace guard and a cat, or that the cat seems to know who I am.

"Many apologies," the guard mumbles. "I thought—"

"You thought *what?*" interrupts the cat named Xyler. "That an unarmed girl poses a grave threat to the kingdom? That you have the right to personally harass distinguished visitors?"

"Of course not. It's just . . . the way she's dressed—"

"Oh, so now you're a *fashion expert?*" Xyler's tail waves angrily back and forth. "If you don't step aside this second, I'll have no choice but to mention this incident to the Royal Family."

The guard nearly drops his spear in his hurry to stagger backward.

"That's better." Xyler struts proudly past him. Along the way, he tosses a glance back at me. "Come along, Kara."

For a moment, I can only stand there like my feet have been superglued to the floor. Then I stumble after him. Once we're far enough away from the guard, I turn a baffled glance in the cat's direction.

"How do you know my name?" I ask.

"Prince Frederick sent me to find you," the cat replies without slowing down. "I've been searching the palace for hours. Then I noticed your scent."

My face reddens as I sniff my armpit. "My *scent?*"

"You smell like Earth." The cat has the same weird pronunciation of the word "Earth" as Prince Fred. Like it's spelled *Urth.* "It's a smell I've encountered before."

"Wait, really? When?"

"That's a story for another time."

"You're right." My voice quavers with urgency. "Can you take me to the Luminary Ball? I need to speak with the prince right away!"

Xyler's eyes flick up at me. "I understand you're eager to attend the party, but that guard was right. You *do* look out of place. Why don't I take you to get a new gown? Something more suited to the occasion. And afterward, we'll have your hair properly groomed. Maybe do something about those nails while we're at it."

"I don't have time for a *makeover*! The prince is in danger."

The cat stops suddenly. "What kind of danger?"

As quickly as I can, I tell him what I witnessed on the balcony. By the time I'm through, the fur is standing up along Xyler's back.

"I never trusted Sturmenburg," he murmurs. "In that case, we have no time to spare. Fortunately, I know a shortcut to the ballroom."

The cat breaks into a run. I race to follow him. Through a room of mirrors. Down a flight of stairs. Along a hall that's decorated with gold-framed paintings of grumpy-looking men and women. They stare out of their canvases with grim expressions, as if they know something bad's about to happen.

Rounding a corner, I catch sight of an arched doorway. Xyler points one white paw. "That's the mezzanine entrance to the Luminary Ball. From there we'll have a better view."

I push through the door. And all of a sudden, my senses are overwhelmed by a dizzying array of lights and music and people. For a long moment, all I can do is stare openmouthed at the vast room. The dance floor is the size of a football field. Every inch is crammed with partiers of all different types. People, elves, dwarfs, fauns. They mingle and dance with each other, while an orchestra plays in the background. Although it's not like any orchestra I've ever seen. Half the instruments seem to be playing *themselves*.

I flinch when a swarm of fireflies darts in front of my vision. Blinking, I realize they aren't fireflies at all. They're fairies. Tiny glowing creatures buzzing through the air on flapping wings. There are at least ten of them, holding a serving tray above them.

"Would you care for a gingerflake, madam?" one of them asks.

"Uh . . . no thanks," I reply.

The serving tray drifts off, and my attention returns to the dance floor. I examine the crowd for a long moment before I see him. Prince Fred. He's standing near the edge of the dance floor. And he's talking with Francesca. After the whole balcony stunt, I should be infuriated by the sight of that psycho snob. But as long as Fred's not hanging out with the grand duke, I'm relieved.

Xyler's perched on the mezzanine railing beside me. He points to an elegant couple below us. A blue-eyed man who looks like an older version of Prince Fred and a beautiful woman with long, blond hair. They're each wearing a crown. I don't need Xyler to tell me who they are.

Prince Fred's parents. The king and queen.

And they're on the opposite end of the ballroom from the prince.

"It's best if we split up," I say. "We'll get to each of them faster."

"Premium idea," the cat replies. "You warn Prince Frederick. I'll notify the king and queen."

At the bottom of the stairs, Xyler and I race off in opposite directions. I push through the crowd, squeezing between clumps of elegantly dressed guests. Before long, I run into a group of dwarfs. They're waiting in the buffet line.

"Sorry! Coming through!" I have to yell to be heard over the blare of music and voices. Meanwhile, the cluster of stout men and women are seriously loading up on the snacks. "Do you mind if I just squeeze past . . . ? No, I don't want a turkey leg. . . . Yes, I'm sure it's delicious, but I can't right now."

At last, I stagger into an opening wide enough to gain a glimpse of Prince Fred. But as soon as I see him, my heart plummets. The grand duke got to him first. The tall, hunched man is locked in conversation with Fred and Francesca. He's holding a goblet in each hand. One's silver; the other's gold.

The Malinwrought must be in one of those cups. I have to get to the prince before he drinks it.

I elbow my way through the clumps of people and fantasy figures. A woman drops her plate. A green-skinned dude growls at me in a language I've never heard before. But I keep moving. There's no time to worry about upsetting the partiers. Not while Prince Fred's on the verge of being poisoned.

Staggering through an opening in the crowd, I catch sight of the prince again. And the moment I see him, a blade of terror cuts through me.

The grand duke has just handed him the golden goblet. Prince Fred raises the cup and presses it to his lips.

Prince Fred

I'm about to take a drink when a bumbling oaf charges into me, knocking the goblet out of my hands and spilling my sparkling honeydrop everywhere. I spin around and realize the bumbling oaf is . . .

Kara?

Finally, she's here. But where has she been? And why did she announce her arrival by running full speed into the Royal Prince in front of a few hundred shocked guests. A gasp goes up throughout the ballroom. The orchestra screeches to a halt. Francesca lets out an outraged "Eeep!" But the person who seems the most upset is the grand duke. His pale eyes flicker back and forth between Kara and the spilled drink. A look of cold rage fills his features.

"You idiot!" he screams at Kara. "What in the seven moons do you think you're doing?"

"Mind your tongue!" My voice comes out harsher than I'd intended. I inhale a deep breath and continue in an even tone. "I'm sure it was an accident."

"But, Your Highness . . ." Sturmenburg can't seem to take his eyes off the spilled drink. "The girl attacked you. We all saw it. She is guilty of treason—"

"Nonsense. That was hardly an attack, Sturmenburg. This is a crowded ballroom. I'm sure she merely lost her footing. Isn't that right, Kara?"

I turn to her. She looks frantic, out of breath. She nods once.

"See?" My attention shifts back to the grand duke. "An innocent mistake. Besides, it's only a little spilled honey-drop. There's plenty more where that came from."

Sturmenburg's gaze hangs on the golden goblet lying sideways on the floor. The edge of his mouth twists with fury.

"Many apologies," he grumbles unapologetically. "I was merely concerned. For your safety."

"And I appreciate that. But I am perfectly safe. You needn't worry." I raise my voice so the crowd of onlookers can hear. "And neither should all of you. This is the Luminary Ball. Back to the celebration!"

And with that, the orchestra strikes up another tune. People return to their dancing and conversation. Crisis averted.

Except Sturmenburg is still obviously upset. And he's not the only one. Francesca is glaring at the newest arrival as though a troll just wandered onto the dance floor.

"How lovely it is to see you again, Kira," she says, even though there's nothing lovely in her tone. Every syllable is muttered through gritted teeth. "I'm *so* glad you could finally make it."

"No thanks to you," Kara mutters. "Now, if you don't mind, I'd like to speak to Prince Frederick. Alone."

Francesca scowls. But it's the grand duke who looks especially outraged. His free hand hovers over his diamond-studded belt, where a diamond-studded dagger is clasped within a diamond-studded sheath.

"And what is it that you'd like to say to His Royal Highness?" he asks coldly.

"I was just wondering . . ."

Kara's eyes dart around the crowded ballroom. Then she takes a steadying breath. Straightening her shoulders, she holds out her hand.

"Your Highness," she says, "would you care to dance?"

Kara

The last thing I want to do right now is bust a move on the dance floor. But it was the only excuse I could come up with. The only way to get some distance from Francesca and the grand duke.

Prince Fred stares at me a long, uncertain moment. I'm sure he has a million reasons to think I've lost my mind. I just barreled into him. I spilled his drink. I probably look like a lunatic.

Francesca isn't even trying to hide her angry sneer.

The grand duke's long fingers inch closer to his diamond-covered dagger.

Then Prince Fred takes my hand and leads me away.

Francesca and the grand duke simmer with fury, but there's nothing they can do to me. Not with so many people around. Not while I'm so close to the prince.

As Fred guides me away, the crowd parts to give us room. I can feel hundreds of eyes following our every movement. Until now, I was always too nervous to even *talk* to guys at school dances. Now here I am, holding hands with the most popular boy in the world.

Literally.

Once we're a safe distance from Francesca and the grand duke, Fred clasps my hand tighter. His arm wraps around me and his fingers settle onto my lower back. The orchestra launches into a new song and his feet begin to move gracefully with the music.

Forward. Forward. Back. Twirl.

He obviously knows what he's doing. I don't. All I can do is shuffle along, trying my best to avoid tripping over my own feet. Or his. And maybe it's the swell of music, or the fairies drifting above us, or my own galloping heart . . . but all of a sudden I feel caught up in the moment. Our hands touching. Our bodies close. Fred's eyes locked on me as he spins me around the ballroom floor. For a flickering instant, it's as if we're just two kids sharing our first dance.

And then reality comes tumbling over me again. Prince Fred's in danger. I'm the only one who can warn him.

I lean in close and whisper into his ear, "That drink the grand duke gave you? Did you swallow any of it?"

Fred gives me a confused look.

"This is serious!" My hand clasps his tighter. "I need to know."

"No," Fred replies. "I didn't have any of the drink."

"Not even a drop?"

"I never got the chance. You knocked the goblet out of my hand."

I'm so relieved, I accidentally stomp on his foot.

"Ow!" Fred yelps.

"Sorry."

"Kara, what's going on?"

As we whirl around the dance floor, I cast a glance around us. Everywhere I look, I see people watching us. Prince Fred's the center of attention. Which also makes *me* the center of attention.

"There's something I need to tell you," I say. "But it's too crowded here. Can we talk somewhere more private?"

Fred's eyebrows knit together. "Now?"

I nod. "It's important."

"Very well."

The prince spins me around and begins to lead us toward the edge of the dance floor. The entire time, he never misses a step. Forward. Forward. Back. Twirl. My palms are sweaty. My feet fumble to keep up. But eventually, we make it to a narrow alcove. A space apart from the crowd.

"All right." Fred gives me a close look. "What's going on?"

The story comes tumbling out. The conversation I witnessed. The grand duke and Hudd plotting to overthrow the Royal Family. The shadow that came to life before my eyes.

"The Sorceress." A shiver grips my voice. "She's still alive. Or at least—some part of her is. She's helping the grand duke poison your parents—"

Fred inhales a sharp gasp.

"It's okay. The talking cat—Xyler—warned them."

I sort of expected Fred to take this news better. Instead of looking reassured, horror creeps across his features. When I follow his gaze, I realize why.

Xyler never reached the king and queen.

I spot the cat at the other end of the ballroom. Clasped in the arms of a guard. Xyler squirms and claws, but it's no use. The guard has him by the scruff of his neck, carrying him away from Fred's parents.

This view is blocked when a tall, hunched figure appears at the edge of the alcove.

"There you are," says the grand duke. "I've been looking all over for you two."

Fred rises to his full height. "My parents. What did you do to them?"

"I have no idea what you're talking about," Sturmenburg says innocently. But there's a sinister gleam in his eyes. "I care only for the safety of the king and queen. That's why I assigned several of my personal guards to ensure that no unauthorized individuals—or animals—come near them. I even delivered their drinks personally ten minutes ago."

The floor drops out beneath me. Peering around the grand duke, I catch a glimpse of Fred's parents. They're standing on a raised platform, happily gazing out at the Luminary Ball. All around them, I see revelers with silver goblets in their hands. But the king and queen have gold goblets.

Exactly like the one Sturmenburg gave to Prince Fred.

A chill slides down my spine as the Royal Couple clink their golden cups together and take a drink.

Every instinct inside me wants to scream, to warn them, to stop them. But it wouldn't do any good. The Malinwrought is already in their systems.

And in three days, the king and queen will be dead.

"My—my parents." Fred's expression goes from horror to fury as he turns his gaze in the grand duke's direction. "You'll never get away with this."

"I'm afraid you're quite wrong about that, Your Highness." The grand duke's tone is equal parts calculating and triumphant, like a chess player who knows he's already won the match. "Soon the throne will be mine. And with the Sorceress at my side, nobody will be able to stop me. At last, I will rule Heldstone."

He takes a step toward us.

"But first, I need to deal with a couple of loose ends." His pale eyes flicker in my direction. "I don't know who you are, little girl, but you've caused enough trouble as it is."

The grand duke blocks our only way out of the narrow alcove.

His cruel gaze lands on Prince Fred. "You should've swallowed the drink I gave you. That would've made all this so much easier."

The grand duke's fingers settle over the dagger's sparkling handle.

"Although this way *is* quicker."

Fred and I stagger backward. Beyond the alcove, the

Luminary Ball is going full steam. A roar of music and voices. But from where we are, it might as well be a million miles away.

Nobody can see us. Nobody can hear us. Nobody knows we're here.

We're trapped. And the grand duke knows it.

His grip tightens on the dagger's handle as he slides it from its sheath.

Prince Fred

The grand duke raises his dagger. But before he can attack, a horrible hiss rips through the ballroom, followed by a bloodcurdling shriek. Sturmenburg spins around. Chaos has broken out behind him. All caused by a single source.

Xyler.

The cat doesn't seem to have been pleased about being carried off the dance floor by one of Sturmenburg's guards. Letting out an awful noise (that was the hiss), he chomped down on the guard's hand (that was the shriek).

Mayhem. The cat whips out of the guard's grip. The guard staggers backward, howling, "That bloody animal just took a bloody bite outta my bloody hand!" A furry shape zigzags between legs and under skirts. Partygoers squeal with shock. A jester on stilts topples into a crowd of very annoyed elves.

For a single stunned moment, all I can do is watch the insanity unfold. Then my attention snaps back to our current situation. The grand duke. The dagger. He whirls back toward us, swinging the blade. But by then, Kara and I are already on the move. We bolt past the grand duke and out of the alcove.

Everyone else is still watching Xyler's mad dash across the dance floor. Or . . . *almost* everyone. A dozen of Sturmenburg's personal guards are waiting for us. I might be the prince, but I have no doubt that these men are loyal to only the grand duke.

"They're getting away!" he calls out. "Don't let them escape!"

The guards raise their weapons. I cast a quick glance in my parents' direction. They're on a raised platform, watching the cat craziness with looks of amusement. They still have no idea of the danger they're in. If I could only reach them, warn them of the treachery inside their own palace. But they're too far away. And Sturmenburg's guards are closing in.

I turn my gaze away from my parents. And instead, it falls on a nearby door.

"Over there!"

I pull Kara by the hand. We tumble through the doorway and into a dim corridor. The walls are lined with flickering torches. Flames snap and hiss. Our shadows tremble all around us.

My heart jumps when I see a guard at the end of the hall. Then I notice the man's uniform. He's not one of Sturmenburg's cronies. He works for the palace. As Kara and I approach, his posture straightens.

"Your Highness?" His voice is thick with surprise. "What's going on?"

I pause long enough to catch my breath. "The Grand Duke Sturmenburg . . . he's trying to kill us."

I peer back the way we came. Shadows leap and swirl against the walls.

The nearest torch suddenly goes out.

A new layer of darkness consumes the corridor.

As the sound of footsteps grows louder, I turn back to the guard. "Sturmenburg's men. They're coming."

The palace guard tightens his grip on his spear. "I shall not allow them to harm you, Your Highness."

But I hardly hear him. All my attention has landed on the wall. A shadow rises up behind the guard. Spreading, growing. I watch, hypnotized with dread, as the shadow takes a human form. And not just *any* human.

The Sorceress.

It's her. Even though her features are pure darkness, I can feel her eyes peering out at me.

Kara was right. The Sorceress is still alive. And she's looming over the guard's back. The dark silhouette emerges from the brick, her arm reaching for the guard.

I open my mouth to warn him, but it's already too late. The shadow grabs the guard. But the Sorceress doesn't stop there. Her fingers vanish inside the man's helmet. A terrible realization hits me. She's reaching *into* the guard's head, grasping hold of his mind with her dark fingers.

All of a sudden, the guard's expression goes blank. His jaw slackens. And then a new look takes hold of his features. It's as though the Sorceress is gazing at me through the guard's eyes.

The guard's lip curls into an evil smirk. And when he speaks, a different voice comes out. The Sorceress's voice.

"Run all you want." Each syllable echoes against the walls of my skull. "But you will never escape me."

The guard's attack arrives like lightning. Before I even realize what's happening, his spear lunges at my chest. I would've been impaled if it weren't for Kara. She tugs my hand, pulling me away from the blade. Steel crashes against the wall. A heartbeat later, Kara and I are on the move again. Racing around a corner and down a narrow hall.

Footsteps and shouts clatter behind us. But it's the shadows that scare me the most. They're everywhere. Climbing the walls. Spilled across the floor. Hanging from the ceiling. In my panic, they all seem alive. As though the Sorceress is everywhere at once.

Turning another corner, we're met by a servant. In front of her is a cart of simmering food. As she bows, her own shadow seems to reach up from the floor. Dark fingers grasping into her forehead. And when the servant rises, her face has gone completely blank.

With astounding quickness, her hand darts into the food cart. And out comes a boiled goose. Kara and I stagger sideways, but we're not quick enough. An instant later, the servant smacks me in the face.

"*Oof!*" I tumble against the wall. All around me, shadows emerge like a thousand hands. Reaching, grasping, pulling. And inside my head, I hear the Sorceress.

"Come to me, Prince Frederick," she whispers. "Abandon this hopeless fight. It will be so much easier that way. Soon it will all be over. Soon, soon, soon . . ."

Her words are like waves lapping against the beach. There's something peaceful about them. I can feel myself giving up the struggle. My arms fall to my sides. My eyelids droop.

Yes, I'll come with you. This thought flows so naturally through my brain. *Take me away from all this trouble. Soon, soon, s—*

"Fred! Snap out of it!"

A new voice slices through my mind. Kara's voice. And I don't like it. Not one bit. It's like a rude servant waking me from a pleasant dream.

Just five more minutes, I think. *Please.*

But Kara's insistent. "You can't let her brainwash you, Fred!" she yells. "Come on! Stay with me!"

It takes a huge amount of effort to open my eyes. When I do, I see Kara. I strain to reach for her, but the shadows are stronger. They yank at me, pulling me backward. And even though Kara's still calling out to me, her words are drowned out by the Sorceress. She's no longer whispering. She's screaming.

"You'll never escape me!" The voice thunders through my brain. "Your kingdom will be mine!"

Kara

The Sorceress is digging around in Prince Fred's brain like it's a candy jar, and there's nothing I can do about it. She's too strong. The shadow has him gripped in an evil bear hug. I can see the light fading from Fred's eyes.

As if that weren't bad enough, a shriek pierces my eardrums. I whirl around just in time to see the servant lady. She's wielding her cooked goose like nunchucks.

With a tight grip on a drumstick, she swings the boiled bird. I barely manage to avoid the blow with a last-second dodge. But before the goose even hits the wall, the servant's already gearing up for her next attack. Her face might be as blank as a statue, but the rest of her is a blur of movement.

She's half servant, half ninja.

I stagger backward. *THWACK!* The goose slams the floor in the exact spot where I'd just been an instant earlier. The servant's too quick. Not to mention the shadows that reach for me whenever I'm too close to the wall. If the Sorceress doesn't brainwash me, I'll end up bludgeoned to death by poultry.

Speaking of . . . here comes the goose again.

WHAM!

The bird slams me in the shoulder. I tumble back into the food cart. Grabbing the handle, I swing it with all my strength. Just as the servant is preparing her next attack, the cart barrels into her. By the time she hits the floor, she's out cold.

I spin back to Prince Fred. He's in even worse shape. The shadows are all around him. Grasping at his neck, wrapped around his legs, reaching into his skull.

I already know what'll happen next. The Sorceress won't bother with brainwashing. Not this time. Not when she's dealing with Prince Fred. She'll do exactly what she did to Hudd earlier. Snatch the life out of his body and leave him dead.

I grab Fred by the shoulders and pull. But the shadow's stronger. It yanks back with stunning force. It's like trying to play tug-of-war with a pickup truck. The prince slips out of my grip. I try again. This time, he doesn't even budge.

"Fred!" I yell. "Listen to me! I can't save you on my own. You have to fight her! Fight the Sorceress!"

His head snaps upward. "K-Kara?" Fred's voice is weak, but it's him. He's still in there.

"Yeah, it's me!" I pull him by the arms. He slumps forward a few inches. "You can do this! Keep fighting! Think about your parents! Only you can save them!"

This seems to make all the difference. Fred's jaw clenches. Sweat pours down his forehead. I can feel his muscles struggling against the Sorceress's magic. And with one last surge of strength, he tumbles out of the shadow's grip.

The two of us immediately break into a sprint. Through a winding corridor, past a mounted boar's head, into a dim room. We stumble to a halt when a guard rounds the corner. His blank expression leaves no doubt—he's already been possessed by the Sorceress.

The man stalks toward us, his gloved hand clasped to the hilt of his sword.

"How many times must I tell you?" The guard speaks, but it's the Sorceress's voice I hear. "Escape is impossible."

A dark shape lands on a cabinet behind him. At first I'm

sure it's just another living shadow. But as the shape gets closer, I realize it's something else entirely.

Not that the guard notices either way. He's too busy spouting out the Sorceress's monologue.

"In three days, the king and queen will be dead," says the brainwashed guard. "But I won't have to wait so long to watch you die."

SHINK! The guard draws his sword. Evil peers out from within his blank features. As he readies his sword, the dark shape slinks along the top of the cabinet. Closer and closer. The guard raises his blade, but before he can attack, the shape launches into the air. A hissing tornado of fur and claws that lands on the man's head.

Screaming and clutching at his face, the guard collapses to the ground. Xyler lands softly beside him.

"You may wish to come with me." He speaks in a calm, formal tone. As if he's inviting us to tea, not helping us escape. "Cats *always* know a shortcut."

Prince Fred

"Xyler! Man, I'm glad to see you!"

Kara picks the cat up off the ground and gives him a tight squeeze. He squirms under her grip.

"Pleasure's all mine," he grumbles. "Now would you please put me down?"

"Sure. Of course." She sets Xyler back on the floor. "You said something about a shortcut?"

The cat nods. "Right this way."

We follow him through a series of hallways. Our mad dash seems to have led us into the servants' quarters. A part of the palace I've never visited before. The accommodations are tighter, dingier. No trace of the opulence I'm accustomed to seeing in the palace.

"Uh . . . Xyler?" I look around. "Where're we going?"

Rather than respond, the cat leaps onto a table. From there, he makes his way to a shelf of neatly organized books. *Proper Polishing of Boots & Slippers. Cooking for the Higher Classes. Greeting Grumpy Guests.* When he reaches the section labeled REMAINING UNSEEN & UNHEARD, he raises a paw and tilts one of the books outward.

CLICK.

All of a sudden, the entire shelf opens like a door. Xyler hops onto the floor and pads softly through the opening. Halfway through, he looks back at me.

"Grab a torch and come with me," he says.

I lift the nearest torch out of its mount and follow Kara through the hidden doorway. She gently slides the shelf closed behind us. The flaming torch illuminates a narrow passageway. Windowless stone walls stretching into darkness.

"What is this place?" I whisper.

Xyler speaks as he guides us forward. "Servants who work in the Royal Palace are expected to accommodate every need and desire of the nobility. And that means being able to move from point A to point B as swiftly as possible— without disturbing any of the distinguished residents."

The cat takes a turn. Kara and I hurry to keep up.

"These passageways were constructed so that servants can move throughout the palace quickly and quietly."

I peer in awe at the tunnels all around us. "I had no idea."

"That was the point. Servants remain invisible and yet ever present."

Xyler leads us down a twisting stairway. Inside the dark space, with nothing but the torch to guide our way, shadows lurk everywhere. All around us. Leaping and surging across the walls, the floor, the ceiling. I swing the torch and the shadows scatter like birds. But shifting the light to one side only increases the darkness on the other. And inside every shadow dwells the potential for evil.

A chill grips my spine. As long as the Sorceress inhabits the palace, I'll never be safe.

"Everything okay?" Kara asks.

I take a deep breath and then nod. "Just a bit spooked."

"Yeah, me too." Kara shivers. "Hey, Xyler. How much farther is it?"

The cat's reply comes from a few steps below. "Almost there."

"Good," Kara and I say at the same time. Then we set off at a quicker pace. Down the stairs. Through another long passageway. Around a corner. Soon we arrive at a steel grate. The bars that once blocked the opening have rusted away. Xyler easily fits inside. Getting onto my hands and knees, I squeeze inside. Kara follows.

"This pipe leads outside the palace walls." Xyler's voice echoes through the tight space from up ahead. "It was once used for disposing raw sewage, but—"

"Wait a moment!" I stop crawling. "You mean this pipe was filled with . . . with . . ."

"*Poop!*" Kara gags. "Ugh! It's a poop pipe!"

"That was a very long time ago," Xyler says. "The palace updated its sewage system two centuries ago. This pipe has been abandoned ever since."

"Oh, so we're crawling through *two-hundred-year-old* poop." Kara casts a revolted look at the curved walls. "Couldn't you have told us that *before* we climbed inside?"

"I was worried you wouldn't follow me," Xyler admits.

"You may be right about that," I say.

"This is the only way we're going to escape the palace without being caught. Although I should probably warn you. We're about to reach a section that can be a bit . . . unpleasant."

"You mean, more unpleasant than mummified poop?" Kara asks.

But Xyler doesn't respond. In fact, when I glance ahead to where he'd just been, the cat seems to be . . .

Gone.

"Xyler?" I call out.

No response.

This doesn't make any sense. A cat can't just ... *disappear*. I crawl forward quickly, searching for any sign of him. Xyler's warning chimes ominously in my mind. *Unpleasant*. What could he have meant by that?

A gust of wind blows through the pipe and my grip on the torch tightens. The flame flaps in the heavy breeze, then flickers out. Everything's consumed in complete darkness.

Confusion and fear unfold inside me. I scramble forward. But before I even realize what's happening, the floor drops out beneath me.

And all of a sudden, I'm falling.

Kara

As if crawling through ancient sewage weren't bad enough. Out of nowhere, everything goes dark. Fred lets out a scream, but the sound of his voice quickly fades. I scramble to follow him. But instead of the floor, my fingers grasp only air. All of a sudden, I topple over and plummet into nothingness.

Down and down and down and—

SPLOOSH!

It's like I've just been dumped out of a waterslide into the swimming pool. I plunge beneath the surface. The cold, dark water jolts me into shock mode. Alarm bells blare in my mind. I can't breathe, can't see, can't tell which way is up. For a few panicked seconds, all I can do is kick and flap my arms wildly. Then I remember what Xyler told us. The pipe leads past the palace walls. Which means we must be outside. I know from my little excursion on the balcony that Heldstone has seven moons. Opening my eyes, I notice their light piercing the darkness. With a few powerful kicks, I see them grow brighter and brighter.

Next thing I know, my head breaks above the surface. Cool air fills my lungs. Wiping the wet hair out of my eyes, the first person I see is Prince Fred.

"Nothing like a little late-night dip, huh?" he says, already paddling toward the shore.

As I climb out of the frigid water, I'm grateful that I'm still holding on to the purse. And the magical owl necklace inside. Without the Chasing Charm, any chance of finding my dad would dwindle to somewhere around zero.

On the shore, I catch sight of a miserable lump of wet fur. Xyler. Seeing the cat fills me with sudden annoyance.

"What happened back there?" My wet shoes squelch as I stomp in his direction. "Don't you think you could've warned us we were about to go for an unexpected swim?"

Xyler stops licking himself and glances at me. "I *said* we were about to experience something unpleasant."

"Maybe next time you can be just a tiny bit more specific.

You know, something like, 'Hey, guys, just a heads-up, but you're about to plunge fifty feet into cold water and you might drown.' Something like *that*."

"My apologies. I fell through the opening before I got the—"

"Shhh." Prince Fred ducks behind a cluster of bushes.

Crouching beside him, I whisper, "What's going on?"

Before he can answer, I hear a faint noise. Footsteps. Peering around the edge of the bush, I spot four guards stalking in our direction.

Nerves twist inside me. What if they heard me doing a massive cannonball a minute ago?

"Any word on the whereabouts of Prince Frederick?" asks one of the guards.

"Still missing," says another. "Grand Duke Sturmenburg saw the prince being abducted by a girl—"

"A girl?"

"Must be how she managed to get so close to the prince. Nobody would suspect a little girl of committing such an act of treason."

One of the guards spits in disgust. "We'll find her. And once we do, she'll get a nice, long stay in the torture chamber before she's killed."

A shudder breaks across my entire body. The footsteps

come to a halt. It sounds like they're just on the other side of the bush. I hold my breath, but my heart keeps pounding.

"Of course, the king and queen are beside themselves with worry," one of them says. "They've canceled the rest of the Luminary Ball and dispatched every last guard and servant to look for Prince Frederick and the girl."

"What if the girl's already left the palace with the prince?"

"The king and queen sent dozens of couriers to alert Royal Guard patrols. And Grand Duke Sturmenburg has personally committed a thousand of his best troops."

"Worry not. By daybreak, the entire kingdom will be searching for the prince. That traitorous girl doesn't stand a chance."

Prince Fred

Once the group of guards finally marches away, I turn a determined glance at Kara. "We must return to the palace at once."

She stares back at me. "You're kidding, right? We barely managed to get out of there. Now you want to go *back?*"

"We have to warn my parents!"

Kara shakes her head. "Didn't you hear what those guys said? I'm, like, at the top of Heldstone's Most Wanted List. If I go anywhere near that palace, they'll arrest me—"

"Not if I tell them the truth. I'm the prince. They *have* to listen to me."

"You already saw how the Sorceress brainwashes people. She can control what they think. It doesn't matter who you are or what you say—if you go back to that palace, we'll *both* be killed."

I cast a frustrated gaze into the moonlit water. As much as I dislike it, Kara's right. There's no way we'll make it far enough into the palace to see Mother and Father. And even if we somehow *did*, the Sorceress could simply climb out of the shadows and reach into their minds, turning them against me.

Kara brings a hand down on my shoulder. "We'll figure out a way for you to see your parents again. I promise."

"What about the poison?" I ask. "In three days—"

She cuts me off before I can say anything more. "There has to be a cure. An antidote. *Something.* We'll find it. And we'll bring it back to them."

I nod, forcing myself to believe her. "The grand duke— the Sorceress . . . they can't get away with this."

"They won't."

A sound from below intrudes on our conversation. Xyler clearing his throat. "Pardon the interruption, but we should probably keep moving."

The cat tilts his head to the right. A cluster of silhouettes in the distance. More guards are headed our way.

Kara opens her soaked purse and unclasps an inner

compartment. Grasping the chain tightly, she removes the Chasing Charm. The little silver owl bursts into the air. Magical metallic wings flapping.

I have no idea where the owl will end up, but I'm certain of what we'll find when we arrive there.

Kara's father.

If we manage to stay alive that long.

I peer out into the dark expanse in front of us. I'm nearly as much of a foreigner in Heldstone as Kara. Practically my entire life was spent inside the palace. On those rare occasions when my parents allowed me outside the walls, I was always surrounded by countless guards.

Gripping the necklace, Kara sets off in the direction that the owl leads her. Xyler follows closely at her heels. I cast one final glance at the palace. My home, looming tall and majestic in the night sky.

I wonder if I'll ever see it again.

Kara

———

The Chasing Charm leads us into the heart of Valpathia, the capital of Heldstone. Once we're there, I carefully place the enchanted owl necklace in the purse and cast a glance at our surroundings. The broad street bustles with men and women and magical creatures. Vendors push rattling carts through the crowd, hollering about their merchandise.

"Half off all drinks! Mead! Cider! Honeydrop!"

"Potions for sale! Buy two, get one free!"

"Clear up your complexion with Auntie Ebb's Enchanted Acne Cream!"

I pull Prince Fred behind a pillar, where we won't be noticed. "Do you have any money?"

"Now isn't the time to purchase acne cream," he says. "Even if it *is* enchanted."

"Not for *that*. You need to buy new clothes. You're not gonna blend into the crowd. Not dressed the way you are."

Fred glances down at his outfit. Everything's still damp from our little swim earlier, but that does little to hide the aristocratic attire. The shiny purple coat, the pearl buttons, the frilly lace poking out of his sleeves. He looks like he should be posing for a royal portrait, not wandering through a street market. Especially when you look at what everyone else is wearing. Drab grays, basic browns. He might as well be wearing a sign on his head that says RUNAWAY PRINCE.

"Perhaps you're right," Fred agrees. "Just one slight problem . . ."

"What?"

Fred stares down at his shoes. "I didn't bring any money."

"Seriously?"

"I left my coin purse in my room. I didn't realize we'd have to make such a quick escape."

I let out a frustrated groan and glance in Xyler's direction.

"Don't look at me," he says matter-of-factly. "Cats have no use for currency."

"My apologies for the oversight," Fred says. "I've never

really been required to carry money. People usually just . . . give me things."

Poor little prince. This snide remark is on the tip of my tongue. But before I can get it out, my attention is snagged by a flicker of gold on Fred's pinky finger. A ring. And it looks expensive.

"Is that real gold?" I ask, nodding to the ring.

A haughty look comes over the prince's expression. "*Of course* it's real gold!"

"Good. Hand it over."

"Now hold on a second." Fred touches the ring defensively. "My father gave this to me. It's been in our family for generations."

"It won't do you much good if you get captured."

"Kara has a point, Your Highness," Xyler says. "Unfortunately, selling the ring could prove difficult because of the Royal Signet—"

"What's a royal signet?"

"An engraving of the Royal Family's coat of arms." Prince Fred holds out his ring. A crest has been carefully carved into the top.

"If Prince Frederick tries to sell his ring," Xyler continues, "then everyone will immediately know it's him. And the whole idea is to *avoid* being recognized."

"Then *I'll* sell it," I say.

Xyler gives this some thought. "Such a rare item *would* fetch a tidy sum on the black market. And with a long journey ahead of us, we *could* use the money—"

"Fine." With a sigh, Prince Fred twists the ring off his pinky and shoves it into my palm. "Just take it."

"I know someone who will purchase the ring without too many questions," Xyler says. "He's a fwarf—"

I tilt a questioning glance at the cat. "What's a fwarf?"

"Half faun, half dwarf. So when you meet him, don't stare." Xyler turns his gaze toward the prince. "It's best if you remain here, Your Highness. We'll return as soon as we can."

Fred nods. "I'm not going anywhere. Have fun with the fwarf."

Xyler leads me quickly through a maze of twisting back alleys. Ancient-looking buildings lean crookedly over cobbled streets. Turning a corner, we meet a stray cat that hisses at us. Xyler replies in a terse tone.

"I just saw a delicious-looking mouse back that way." He points a paw behind us. "If you go now, you might be able to catch it."

The stray cat lets out an excited meow and bolts off in one direction. We go in the other.

A minute later, we emerge into a dingy square. Masses

of people swarm through a chaos of dirty-looking tents and cobbled-together wooden booths. Smoke and raucous shouts fill the air. A groggy group spews from the open door of a dilapidated shack. It's impossible to tell whether they're best friends or about to break into a fistfight. Maybe both.

I turn an uncertain glance down at Xyler. "You sure *this* is the best place to sell the ring?"

"Unfortunately, yes. The black marketplace might be unruly and dangerous—"

"And stinky." I pinch my nose.

"But it's also the epicenter of illegal activity in Valpathia."

"Well, that's comforting."

"Merchants here are much less likely to alert the Royal Guard when someone tries to sell them stolen goods."

"Fine." I tighten the grip on my purse. My most valuable possession is inside. "Let's just get this over with."

Xyler leads the way through the chaotic mob. Most of the people here are too busy with their own shady dealings to even notice us. A fairy wobbles unsteadily through the air. A dark figure in a robe approaches us, muttering something about "deadly potions at steep discounts."

"Uh, no thanks," I say, staggering to catch up with Xyler.

The cat weaves through the crowd, eventually ending up at a tent. Pausing at the front flap, he looks back at me.

"It's probably best if I do the talking."

Following Xyler into the tent, I take in my surroundings: Stained burlap walls. Boxes open to display glittering jewelry. Wooden crates stacked in one corner. Framed paintings in another.

"No children allowed!"

The shrill, screechy voice takes me by surprise. An instant later, one of the paintings swivels and I notice the figure holding it. This must be the fwarf. The guy barely reaches my chest. And that includes the horns that poke out of his curly brown hair. For a split second, I think he must be wearing a pair of fur pants. But nope—those are his legs.

"Get out!" the fwarf commands. "This isn't a nursery. I don't look after lost children."

Xyler speaks up. "She's with me."

The little furry-legged man's eyes drop to the floor. "Xyler! Didn't see you there."

"Hello, Percival. It's been a while."

"Quite a while. To what do I owe the pleasure?"

"There's something we'd like to show you. A spectacular object. Truly one of a kind."

Xyler gives me a quick look. That's my cue. Opening my hand, I show Percival the gold ring glimmering in my palm.

The fwarf—Percival—gingerly sets down the painting and steps across the tent. His hooves click against the stone floor. He plucks the ring out of my hand and studies it with his dark eyes.

"This is the royal signet," he murmurs. "An exceedingly rare piece. If it's not a forgery."

"I assure you, the ring's authentic," Xyler replies calmly.

"We shall see about that." Percival fishes in his pocket and removes a magnifying lens. Holding the ring in front of the lens, he turns it one way, then the other, muttering to himself. "Engraving's at least two centuries old. Yet the coat of arms remains remarkably intact. Unparalleled craftsmanship."

Returning the lens to his pocket, he slowly shifts his dark eyes from Xyler to me. He seems to be examining us the same way he examined the ring. Closely, skeptically, coldly. As his attention lands on me, I feel my skin prickle.

"This is quite a unique item, little lass," he says. "How did it come into *your* possession?"

Before I can speak, Xyler answers for me. "She works in the palace."

Without taking his focus off me, without even blinking, the fwarf replies, "I asked the girl, Xyler. Not you."

Percival inches closer. Any second now, I'm sure he's going to pull out his magnifying lens and start inspecting *me*.

"Well, little lass?" He raises an eyebrow. "How'd you get this pretty ring?"

I straighten my shoulders, forcing myself to reply in my most confident tone. "I'm not telling."

Now both of Percival's eyebrows are raised. "Is that so?"

I nod. "My lips are sealed."

"I'm not buying this ring until you tell me how you got your hands on it."

The fwarf's harsh gaze burns into me. But I don't back down. I can't say exactly why. It's just a feeling. A glimmer of an idea at the corner of my mind.

"You want to sell your ring, right?" Percival whispers. "So just tell me how you obtained it."

"No." The word comes out firm as stone. "I'm not telling. Ever."

"I see." Percival backs away, rubbing his chin thoughtfully.

Xyler lets out a nervous chuckle. "The girl's obviously confused. If I could just speak with her for a moment alone, I'm sure—"

"That won't be necessary," Percival interrupts. "I'll buy the ring."

Xyler's ears prick up in surprise. "You—you will?"

"Indeed I will."

"But . . . you said—"

"I know what I said. And despite my threats, the girl refused to back down. That tells me she can keep a secret."

The fwarf holds the ring up to the light of a candle admiringly.

"If I'm going to acquire such a unique object, I need to know the girl won't blab to the wrong person. Otherwise, the Royal Guard's gonna start poking their noses into my business, asking about missing rings. Can't have that, now, can we?"

"No, you most certainly cannot." Xyler gazes up at me like he's seeing me for the first time.

I let the two of them handle the negotiations. Once they come to an agreement, Percival drops several gold coins into a small velvet bag.

"Pleasure doing business with you," he says, pressing the bag into my hand.

As we exit the tent, I feel like doing a celebratory fist pump. My first shady business deal with a half dwarf, half faun! Not exactly the kind of thing I'll be able to put on my college applications someday, but still—it's exciting.

Xyler grumbles that we got ripped off. "The value of that ring is far greater than what he paid us," he complains. But it's more than enough for what we need.

When we return to our hiding place, my triumphant mood takes a nosedive. There's no sign of Prince Fred. Xyler and I glance around, tendrils of confusion and fear creeping into my brain. Then my attention gets snagged by a flicker of movement from a nearby alleyway. A hand waving at us. As we approach, Fred pokes his head around a corner.

"Finally! What took you so long?" His voice comes tumbling out in a frantic whisper. "The Royal Guard. They were sniffing around everywhere. Nearly spotted me. Had to find a new place to hide. I was worried you'd been captured or killed or—"

"It's okay." I place a steady hand on Fred's shoulder. "We're fine."

The prince shakes his head. "We're most certainly *not* fine. I overheard a couple of guards. They said they've set up checkpoints at every city gate. Valpathia has been sealed off."

A grim look clouds his features.

"There's no way out of the city," he says. "We're trapped."

Prince Fred

The awful reality of our situation hangs over us like a dark cloud. If we can't leave Valpathia, we have no chance of finding her father. Or of seeing my parents again.

"We have to at least *try*." Desperation clings to Kara's voice. "There's gotta be a way out. We just have to keep looking."

She stuffs a clump of brown fabric into my arms. My disguise. I find a private section of the alley and change. The new attire is drab. The scratchy material makes me feel like I'm wearing a potato sack. But at least I no longer resemble a prince.

When I step around the corner, I find Kara waiting for

me in her own new outfit. A brown dress, with a matching scarf to conceal her hair.

She looks like she just stepped off a farm. I probably look the same.

In our new clothing, we scurry through the dark, winding alleyways of Valpathia. Turning a corner, Kara comes to an abrupt halt. We duck behind a barrel, and she points to the street ahead. A patrol of Royal Guards. They've set up a checkpoint at one of the city gates. We turn and take another route, but the result is the same.

Another checkpoint. More guards.

"It's just as I feared." I let out a frustrated breath. "The streets are closed."

"Then perhaps we should travel *above* the streets," Xyler says.

I glance at the cat. "What do you mean?"

"Humans are always keeping their feet on the ground. You forget there are other ways of getting from one place to another."

"You're talking about crossing the city . . . by rooftop?"

Xyler nods. "The path will be more difficult. But if you move quickly, Sturmenburg's troops won't be looking for you there."

He guides us silently away from the guards. Until we

reach a stone house at the end of the alley. Crimson ivy clings to one wall. Without a word, Xyler clambers up.

I turn to Kara. "Have you ever done anything like this before?"

"My mom sometimes takes me to the climbing wall." She shrugs. "Can't be harder than that, right?"

And with surprising skillfulness, she skitters to the roof. When my turn comes around, I feel much more awkward. Grabbing a handful of ivy, I try to pull myself up. Instead, the leaves rip loose from the wall and I tumble backward.

Kara peers down at me. "Use the vines underneath. They're thicker and they make good handholds."

I take her advice, and my second attempt goes much better. Digging my hands beneath the clusters of leaves, I grab hold of the ropy vines that cling to the wall, using them like a ladder for my hands and feet. Up and up and up. Slinging my leg over the top, I pull myself onto the roof.

"Now what?" I ask.

"We'll travel west." Xyler points. A jumble of rooftops stretches like a quilt under the moonlight. "If we stay above street level, we should be able to avoid the Royal Guard's checkpoints. Just remember—people are sleeping beneath us. So tread lightly."

Xyler moves silently to the edge of the building. I try to mimic his soft steps, but I'm not a cat. Stealth isn't my strong suit. Roof tiles clatter quietly under my feet. I only hope the sound isn't as noticeable for whoever's snoozing down below.

The stone house is separated from the next building by a narrow alley. Xyler leaps over the gap and lands on the opposing rooftop.

I glance uncertainly at Kara. "Have you ever done *this* before?"

"Coach Peterson makes us do long jump in PE," she says. "Does that count?"

I exhale a jealous sigh. Why don't we have climbing walls and PE in Heldstone?

Kara manages the leap from one roof to the next. Now I'm the only one left standing on the stone house. As I peer over the edge, all I can think about is the fall. The journey ahead is difficult enough already. It'll be impossible with a broken leg or two.

"You can do this," Kara says in a quiet voice from the next rooftop. "I know you can."

The confidence in her voice helps distract me from the knot of fear in my stomach. I take two steps backward. Deep breath. And before the doubt can creep back into my brain, I surge forward and—

Jump.

Somewhere between the two buildings, my heart skips a beat. But in the next instant, my feet make contact with the roof. I did it! And from there, it gets easier. Xyler leads the way. From one building to another. One rooftop to another. Keeping low to avoid being seen by anyone on the street below. Until eventually, we arrive at a house on the edge of the city.

Xyler glances over the edge of the roof. "This should be far enough. The Royal Guard won't have any checkpoints out here."

We climb down a drainage pipe. As my feet land on soft dirt, I peer into the darkness. In the distance, I can just barely see the walls that surround Valpathia on all sides.

We made it outside the city. But we still have a long way to go.

Kara unclasps the inner compartment of her purse and out springs the little silver owl. The Chasing Charm flaps its metal wings, darting into the air from one end of the necklace. Kara keeps a tight grip on the other.

The owl's beak points west. We set off in that direction.

Kara

It feels like we've been walking for hours. My entire body is weak from exhaustion and hunger. But every time I'm sure I can't take another step, I think of my dad. The sound of his voice. The way he always called me *hija*. Spanish for "daughter." His smile, which made every lightbulb in the room burn a little brighter. All the tiny, huge things that have been missing from my life for these past three years.

The only way I'll ever have a chance of seeing him again is if I keep moving. One foot in front of the other. Following the path of the owl necklace.

So I keep walking. And walking.

And walking.

Fred and Xyler trudge along beside me. My sore feet stumble over mud and rocks. I've never been so hungry in my life. Or so tired. I catch myself fantasizing about drifting off to sleep on a bed of hamburgers and french fries.

When I'm sure I'm about to collapse, I notice a shape in the darkness. As we stagger closer, I can see it more clearly. Fred has obviously spotted it, too. He points a finger.

"Look there." His voice comes out as a weak croak. "A farmhouse."

"There's a stable beside it," I add. "Maybe we can spend the night there."

We creep toward the farmhouse. The windows are dark and there's no smoke coming from the chimney. Anyone inside has probably been asleep for hours. As we approach the stable, I peer through the open doors. The place looks vacant. Just a few stalls, a barrel, piles of hay—

"Moo!" A cow pokes its head out from one of the stalls.

Okay, so the stable isn't entirely vacant after all.

The cow takes a few steps in our direction, peering at us with its big, bovine eyes. Then it opens its mouth and speaks in a gentle female voice.

"May I help you?"

For a long moment, all I can do is stare. I've never had a conversation with a cow before.

Luckily, Fred's not so new to this kind of thing. "We're terribly sorry for disturbing you so late at night," he says. "And for intruding on your home. My name is Pr—"

The prince catches himself before blurting out his full name and title. After another second, he continues.

"My name is . . . Fred. And these are my friends Kara and Xyler."

The cat and I wave hello. The cow introduces herself as Gerta.

"We've been traveling a long time without food or rest," Fred continues. "When we saw this stable, we thought . . . well—"

"You thought you might stay the night?" Gerta suggests.

"Precisely."

"The farmer and his wife live in the house. They wouldn't like the idea of uninvited guests in their stable. Not at all." Gerta pauses, considering us. "I, on the other hand, could use the company. It's not the most luxurious lodging, but there's a roof over our heads and plenty of hay to sleep on. Just make sure you leave before the farmer and his wife wake up."

I've never wanted to hug a farm animal so much in my entire life. "Thank you!"

"Don't mention it. It'll be nice to have others around. It's been so lonely in this stable since . . ."

Gerta goes quiet suddenly. Her brown eyes hang for a long moment on a wooden box near the entrance to the stable. It's twice my height, filled with rows of cages. Wire mesh covers each opening. Feathers are scattered along the floor of each cage, but there's no sign of any birds.

"Is that a chicken coop?" I ask, pointing to the box of cages.

Gerta nods.

"But where are all the chickens?"

"For a long time, they shared this stable with me. Their constant clucking could get annoying, but they were nice birds. And then one day . . ." Gerta hesitates. "One day, they—uh . . . migrated south for the winter."

I blink, confused. I don't know much about the migration patterns of chickens, but the answer sounds like a lie to me.

"Er—let's get on with the tour . . . ," Gerta says quickly, as if she's eager to change the subject. "There's a well at the top of the hill for water. And the window around back doesn't lock properly. It leads to the kitchen, where you should be able to find some leftover bread and cheese."

At the mention of food, I forget all about the missing chickens. My stomach lets out a rumbling growl.

"The farmer and his wife are deep sleepers," says Gerta. "As long as you're quiet, they won't notice you."

"But don't you think they'll mind us taking their food?" I ask.

"The farmer's wife will buy fresh bread at the market tomorrow. And technically, *I'm* the reason they have the cheese." Gerta bats her eyelashes. "And I grant you my permission to sample it."

Gerta's explanation is good enough for me. Fred and I set off on our late-night kitchen raid. We offer to bring something back for Xyler, but he shakes his head. "I ate a juicy beetle on the way here." The cat pats his belly. "Very filling."

Sure enough, the window's been left unlocked. Fred swings it open and we slip inside. After searching around in the dark, we manage to find bread and cheese. By the time we return to the stable, Xyler's fast asleep. So's Gerta. Fred and I settle down on a spot of grass outside the stable.

With our backs against the wooden wall, we spread out our food on the ground in front of us. Sort of like a picnic. The bread's hard and the cheese doesn't taste like what my mom buys at the grocery store, but I'm way too hungry to care. For a few minutes, neither of us says a word. We're too busy stuffing our faces.

Eventually, Fred wipes the crumbs from his lap and looks up at the night sky. "Do you know why the Luminary Ball takes place tonight of all nights?"

I shake my head.

"Because of *that*." He points upward. An array of moons hanging in the night sky like perfectly round lamps. "Seven full moons on the same night. An occurrence that only comes along once every seven years. And so we celebrate it."

"With the Luminary Ball."

"Precisely."

A faint smile pulls at my lips. "Guess I'm lucky I was here to see it."

"Too bad the rest of your visit *hasn't* been so lucky." He pulls a blade of grass from the ground and twists it between his fingers. "It's a shame, really. Makes me wish . . ."

His voice is swallowed by the wind.

"Wish *what*?" I ask.

"That we could've met under more normal circumstances. You know, without all the craziness surrounding our lives. Like the fact that you come from another world—"

"Or that you're a prince," I point out.

"Or that we're being hunted by an evil shadow and her army."

Neither of us says a word for a minute. We just listen to the breeze and the soft snores of Gerta from inside the stable.

"Who knows?" I shrug. "Maybe someday everything *will* be normal. And we can get together and just hang out. You know, like typical kids."

"Do you really think that's possible?"

I peer up at the night sky. "I'm in another world, next to a real-life prince, looking up at *seven* full moons. So, yeah. I'd say, pretty much *anything* is possible."

For a long time, Fred and I sit there in silence, staring out at the bright moons. They seem at once far away and close enough to grasp in the palms of our hands.

It's a beautiful view. A magical view. No matter what else happens on this quest, I'm glad Fred's here to share it with me.

If only I could hang on to the moment longer. But it's late. And after the day we've had, we're both experiencing some serious inter-dimensional jet lag.

Returning to the stable, Fred and I shuffle tiredly into neighboring stalls.

"Big day tomorrow," I say. "See you in the morning."

"Sleep tight," he replies. "Don't let the bed fairies bite."

All I have underneath me is a thin layer of hay and hard wooden slats, but it might as well be a king-sized feather bed. In less than a minute, I drift into a dreamless sleep.

When my eyes open again, light's streaming through

the stable. I let out a massive yawn, rising to a sitting position. That's when a shadow shifts across the floor. Glancing behind me, I'm met with a sight that wakes me up faster than a cold shower.

There's a stranger in the stall with me. A stout lady in an apron. And she's poking a pitchfork in my face.

Prince Fred

"Well, lookie here. We got a coupla vagrants sleepin' in the stable."

These are the first words I hear when I wake up the next morning. Opening my eyes, I'm met by a most unpleasant sight: a large, hairy man glowering down at me. He's gripping a shovel as if it's an ax.

This must be the farmer. The man prods me up with his shovel and marches me into another stall, where Kara's been cornered by a plump woman with a pitchfork. She must be the farmer's wife.

The pointy end of the farmer's shovel pokes me in the back. I stagger forward until I'm standing next to Kara.

Glancing around, I don't see any sign of Xyler or Gerta.

It's just the two of us.

And the two adults.

"This is no charity inn." The farmer's wife eyes us suspiciously. "You younguns are trespassin'."

Leaning forward on her pitchfork, the farmer's wife inspects me more closely. For a torturous moment, I'm sure she'll recognize my true identity. But the expression in her eyes makes it clear—she has no idea I'm the prince. Neither does her husband. To them, I'm just a common boy with grit on my face and hay in my hair.

"We're very sorry for the intrusion," I say, doing my best to hide my highborn accent. "Can't you please just let us go?"

The farmer shakes his head firmly. "'Fraid not. You younguns committed a crime. And crimes gotta be punished."

"But . . ." Kara's voice trembles. "We won't do it again. Promise."

"Save yer excuses fer the soldiers," the farmer replies.

A strain of fear needles into my brain. It doesn't matter whether these two don't recognize me. The soldiers *will*. My muscles twitch with the impulse to escape. But the adults are blocking any path out of the stall, gripping their tools close.

"Please." I turn my desperate gaze from the farmer to his wife. "We have money. We can pay."

"Too late fer that," the farmer replies.

"Isn't there *something* we can do?" Kara asks.

"Well, now thatcha mention it . . ." The farmer's wife exchanges a crafty glance with her husband. "One thing *does* come to mind."

"There's a problem that needs to be fixed," says the farmer. "If you help us with it, we'll let you go free."

Kara and I both nod eagerly.

"We'll do it!" she says.

"Absolutely!" I say.

Perhaps we answered too quickly. Because as soon as the farmer and his wife explain the task, it becomes perfectly obvious.

Their problem is probably going to get us killed.

Kara

The farmer and his wife lead us across the stable. And just in case either of us has any ideas about escaping, they keep their weapons raised and ready. The pitchfork jabs dangerously close to my side. Fred yelps when the farmer pokes him in the shoulder with the shovel.

"Keep movin'," grunts the farmer.

Fred and I scramble forward until we reach the chicken coop. I remember wondering last night: why were all the cages empty?

Well, now they're not all empty.

Because Xyler is locked inside one of the cages.

"We found yer feline friend," growls the farmer's wife. "Tried to bite me while I was lockin' 'im up."

Her husband prods the cage with his shovel. "Last week, this entire coop was full a chickens. Then one mornin', they were gone."

"Every last one of 'em," says the woman.

"What happened?" I ask.

The farmer glares at the empty cages. "They were stolen. By a troll."

At least now I know why Gerta was being so mysterious about the empty coop last night. The cow must've wanted us to believe that the chickens migrated south for the winter because the truth was much scarier.

There's a troll chicken thief on the loose.

And as if that's not bad enough, the farmer and his wife have even worse news.

"We can't have that monster rampagin' our farm," the man says through gritted teeth.

"Which is why we want you kids to kill it," says his wife.

It's a good thing I'm already leaning against the wall. Otherwise, I'm pretty sure I'd be lying on my back right now.

"We . . . we're only kids." Fred sounds like he's just as freaked out. "How are we supposed to kill a troll?"

The farmer's wife shrugs. "That's fer you to figure out."

"Otherwise, I'll march the two a you vagrants down to the nearest barracks," says the farmer.

The idea of facing off against a troll might be terrifying, but it's not as bad as being captured. We were lucky to make it out of the palace once. If we're marched back there in chains, we'll never get out again.

"We'll do it." I take a deep breath, steadying my voice. "We'll kill the troll."

The farmer grins, revealing a mouthful of rotten yellow teeth. "Good. And just in case you think about runnin' off before the job's done, we'll hang on to yer cat." He rattles Xyler's cage. "Fer safekeepin'."

⌒

Fred and I wander through a field of tall grass, trying to come up with an idea.

"How in the seven moons are we going to do this?" he asks.

"Don't ask me." I kick a clump of hay. "I've never even *met* a troll before. Now I'm supposed to *kill* one?"

I give the hay another fierce kick. Our task is hopeless.

"Moo."

Fred and I whirl around to see Gerta approaching.

"I'm so sorry about all this," says the cow. "The farmer

and his wife don't usually come to the stable so early. I suppose they've been paranoid lately because of the chickens—"

"You mean the chickens that got *stolen?*" I interrupt. "By a *troll?*"

"Why'd you lie to us?" Fred stares at Gerta, hands on his hips. "Why didn't you just tell us what really happened?"

Gerta shakes her head sadly. "I . . . I couldn't. I made a promise."

"A promise?" Fred asks. "To whom?"

But instead of answering, the cow darts her eyes past us. Following her gaze, I spot the farmer. He's stomping our way.

Gerta's attention snaps back to us. "There isn't much time. You must listen. I can help."

You already lied to us once, I think. *Why should we trust anything you say?*

But I swallow my skepticism. Whatever Gerta's about to say, it's obviously important. We might as well hear her out. "The farmer will offer you weapons," says the cow. "But they won't do you any good against the troll."

"Well, that's just great," I mutter. "Like we didn't have enough reasons to be afraid already."

"If you want to defeat the troll, there's only one thing you'll need," Gerta says.

"What's that?"

"Cheese."

It takes my brain a split second to catch up with what the cow just said. I'm sure I must've misheard her.

"Hold on. Did you just say . . ." I let out an astounded breath. "*Cheese?*"

Gerta nods.

Even in our dire situation, I can't hold back my sarcasm. "Any particular *kind of* cheese you'd recommend? Cheddar? Swiss? String?"

The farmer's footsteps clomp through the grass, heading toward us. Gerta casts a quick glance at him, then turns her pleading eyes back on us.

"I know how crazy it sounds," she says. "But you must do it. When the farmer gets here, come up with an excuse—"

"I hate to break up the conversation." The farmer clomps up to us, showing off his rotten grin. "But I believe you kids have a troll to kill. We don't have much in the way of weapons round the farm, but I can offer you my shovel. Or maybe a kitchen knife?"

"We don't need any weapons," Fred replies.

I shoot him a nervous look. Is he really going along with Gerta's plan?

The farmer's forehead wrinkles. "No weapons? You sure 'bout that?"

Fred's face has gone pale, but he doesn't change his

mind. "Yes. We're sure. Although—uh . . . it might be difficult to face a troll on an empty stomach. If you would see fit to feed us before we depart, we would appreciate it."

The farmer runs a hand through his hair. "I s'pose a bit a breakfast couldn't hurt. What were you thinkin'?"

Even as the words come out of my mouth, I can't believe what I'm saying. "Do you have any cheese?"

A few minutes later, the farmer returns with a block of cheese. As he approaches, he points toward the rocky hill that looms over the farm like a long, jagged claw. Near the top is a cave.

"See that cave?" he says. "That's where you'll find the troll. Don't return till it's dead. And we expect to see proof that the job's done."

He shoves the cheese into my hands.

"Good luck."

And so the prince and I set out. Up the steep, stony incline. Navigating our way between massive boulders and the sharp branches of long-dead trees.

Higher and higher and higher.

Inside my chest, my heart's hammering. Although I'm not sure whether that's because of the tough climb or the dread pulsing inside me. Maybe both.

Emerging from behind a cluster of boulders, Fred and I stumble to a halt. There it is, right in front of us.

The cave.

For a long moment, all we can do is stare into the vast opening. A thick, murky darkness looms inside.

"I guess this is the place," Fred mumbles in a soft, shaky voice.

"Guess so." I stare into the dark mouth of the cave, fear swirling in my stomach. "You sure about this?"

Fred hesitates. "No."

"Me neither."

I'm about to suggest we turn back. There has to be another way. Another chore we can take care of around the farm. Something with a slightly lower chance of being horribly killed. But before I can get the words out, a noise echoes from deep within the cave.

"ROOAAAAARRRR!"

The sound rattles my rib cage. Every cell of my body wants to run, but my knees have turned to jelly. I doubt I'd make it ten feet before collapsing into a terrified heap.

A movement stirs the darkness inside the cave. Massive footsteps shake the ground beneath me.

An instant later, the troll emerges.

Prince Fred

The troll is twice as tall as even the tallest man. Built like a boulder, with a massive stomach and hands that could crush your skull like a grape. Its skin is a sickening shade of green. Its feet clobber the ground with each step.

Standing at the edge of the cave, the troll opens its mouth to release another thunderous roar.

I feel my last glimmer of courage flicker away. Beside me, Kara shivers like a leaf in the wind. I wouldn't be surprised if she turned and fled. Instead, her fingers tighten around our secret weapon.

The block of cheese.

She raises the cheese above her head. And in a loud,

trembling voice, she calls out, "W-we . . . b-brought this for you!"

A look of utter astonishment falls over the troll's big green face. Its black eyes peer at the cheese in Kara's hands. When it opens its mouth, I'm expecting another bone-rattling roar. But what comes out instead is a gentle, squeaky voice.

"You . . . You brought me . . . cheese?"

Kara's head bobs up and down once. "Yes."

"No sharp pointy things? Or hard clobbering things? Or flaming hot things?"

Kara's head shakes back and forth once. "No."

"Does that mean that . . . you're *not* here to hurt me?"

Well, actually we've been sent to kill you. These words hang heavy in my mind. But I keep them to myself. Even though the troll is enormous and scary looking, there's something in his soft, curious voice. Something childlike. Something that makes me think he's just as uninterested in bloodshed as we are.

And so I raise my own voice, and I reply: "We mean you no harm. We're just here because—well . . . because of some missing chickens."

The rest of the story comes pouring out. Kara and I take turns telling the troll about how we spent the night in the stable. How we were discovered by the farmer and his wife. And about the terrible task they assigned us.

The troll listens in silence. Once we're done, he seems relieved.

"I just want to apologize for all the scary roaring earlier," he says. "Most people have a pretty low opinion of trolls. They show up at my cave to yell and throw things. I'd rather frighten them off before the situation gets violent."

I stare at the giant green monster, too stunned to respond. I had no idea a troll could be so . . . un-troll-like.

"So I'm guessing you didn't eat the chickens?" Kara asks.

"Of course not." The troll seems repulsed by such an idea. "I don't even eat meat."

Kara's jaw drops. "You're . . . a vegetarian?"

"I suppose you could call it that."

"But then . . . what happened to the chickens?"

"I'll show you." The troll steps back, gesturing into his cave. "Come inside. I have some jelly that will pair nicely with that cheese."

This isn't how I expected events to turn out, but it's certainly better than having our heads ripped off.

Kara and I follow the troll into his cave. Along the way,

he introduces himself as Groosel. "But my friends call me Groo," he adds. "So you can call me Groo, too."

Trailing behind him, I stare in awe at my surroundings. This cave is nothing like what I'd imagined. Homemade candles hang from the ceiling, casting a soft glow across the space. A layer of moss has been laid over the ground like a fuzzy green carpet. Framed portraits of somber-looking trolls gaze out from the walls.

Groo gestures to our well-furnished surroundings. "Just because I live in a cave doesn't mean it shouldn't feel like home."

"It's gorgeous." Kara stops to admire a crackling fireplace that's been carved into the stone. "Do you live here alone, or do you have—uh . . . cavemates?"

"I'm the only troll here." Groo lets out a heavy sigh. "My family and I used to live in a troll settlement just beyond the Borndal Mountains. We had a good life there. Unfortunately, not all trolls shared our commitment to nonviolence. There were attacks against my family, and . . ."

Groo's voice trails off. His dark eyes land on a framed painting of a female troll. Dark hair hangs around her pale green face. Maybe she was his sister. Or his wife. Either way, Groo obviously misses her.

"I was the only one who made it out alive," he says in a

strained voice. "I thought maybe I could live in a human village instead. But that didn't work out so well, either. Half the villagers wanted to kill me. The other half wanted to enslave me. Once again, I had to flee. And from then on, I knew—if I wanted to live in peace, I had to live apart from society. Away from humans. And other trolls."

"Don't you get lonely?" Kara asks.

"Oh, but I'm not alone. Come on, I'll show you."

The ground trembles beneath us as Groo stomps deeper into the cave. Kara and I follow him. Along the way, we take in the sights. There's a sofa carved from stone. And a wooden tube that runs from the ceiling, channeling rainwater into a barrel. A basket on the counter contains a huge pile of eggs.

Parting an ivy curtain, Groo introduces us to yet another surprise.

His cave comes with a backyard.

The stone walls open up to reveal a vast, hidden valley deep within the tall, craggy hill. Light pours in through a gap in the rocky ceiling, shining down on a meadow of tall grass and bright flowers. A stream trickles under an opening in the stone. Orderly rows of crops—corn, wheat, lettuce—have sprouted across one side of the yard. And wandering through all of this, pecking and flapping and squawking, are several dozen . . .

Chickens.

Groo gestures to the birds. "See what I mean? I'm not alone here after all."

A look of realization flashes across Kara's features. "You had no intention of killing the chickens. You wanted to give them a home."

Groo nods. "The farmer and his wife kept them under miserable conditions. Locked inside crowded cages. Unable to roam around. It was chicken abuse. So I did the only ethical thing. I rescued them. Brought them here, where they can have a better life. I provide them with an open, happy environment. And they provide me with eggs."

Lumbering into the meadow, Groo tosses giant handfuls of seed to the mob of excited chickens. I think back on all the awful things I've heard about trolls over the years. That they're brainless monsters. Beasts that destroy entire villages. Savages.

Groo disproves all that.

"Only Gerta knows what really happened to those chickens," he says. "And she promised she wouldn't tell anyone."

"That explains why she lied to us," I say. "But why the secrecy?"

"Because." Groo lets out a heavy sigh. "The truth could

get me killed. The only thing keeping humans away is fear. They think I'm a brutal monster. I can't let them find out I'm—"

"A vegetarian with a free-range chicken farm?" Kara suggests.

Groo nods ruefully. "Once they discover the truth, they won't fear me. And if they don't fear me, they'll come after me with sharp pointy things and hard clobbering things and flaming hot things."

I shudder at the thought that humans can be so cruel. But of course we can. I've seen plenty of evidence to prove it lately.

Casting a glance around at Groo's hidden paradise, I say, "We won't tell anyone about this place."

"Or about you," Kara adds.

The troll gazes down at us gratefully. "Thank you."

"But we still have a problem." I dig my hands into the pockets of my cloak. "The farmer and his wife. If they don't get evidence of your death, they'll have us arrested."

The troll scratches behind his big green ear. "I've been thinking about that. And I might have an idea that can fix both our problems."

"What's that?"

He gives us a steady look. "I want you to kill me."

Kara

The three of us sit down at an enormous stone table in the cave's dining room. In front of us is a platter of cheese and jelly. "Plus some of my delicious homemade bread," Groo adds. As we eat our breakfast, the troll explains his plan.

"It's simple, really," he says between bites of cheese. "The farmer and his wife want me dead. So that's what we'll give them. A death scene."

"But . . ." Fred's eyebrows knit together. "How?"

"We'll fake it."

"Do you think they'll believe that?"

"Sure. As long as we put on a good show." Groo pops a

giant piece of bread into his mouth. "You said they want proof, right? Well, why not let them witness my death for themselves?"

I gaze up at the troll, impressed. "This could actually work."

"Everyone gets what they want," he says. "The farmer and his wife will believe the big, bad monster is gone. You kids can go free. And if the humans think I'm dead, they won't show up at my cave, trying to kill me." With the sound of clucking chickens in the background, we work through the rest of the details. By the time we're done with breakfast, the plan's in place.

"Let's go." Groo presses his massive hands against the table, rising from his seat. "We have a death to fake."

The three of us hike down the hill until we reach a flat section with a perfect view of the farm below. It's the ideal spot for a staged fight. Close, but not *too* close. We want the farmer and his wife to see everything that happens, without being able to tell none of it is real.

It's a lot like a school play. We even have props. Groo lumbers behind us, carrying a giant lump of moss that's been stitched and tied into just the right form. Fred's holding a flaming torch. And I have a big rock that I found outside Groo's cave.

Once everyone's in their positions, Groo stands at the

edge of an overhang and releases a horrendous roar. The noise echoes across the valley below. Just as we'd hoped, Groo's sound effect gets the attention of the farmer and his wife. They come stumbling out of the house, peering up the hill in the troll's direction. Even from a distance, I can see the revulsion and terror in their faces.

Near the stable, I catch sight of Gerta. When she spots Groo, she lets out a surprised "Moo."

We have our audience. Now it's time to put on the big show.

Groo whirls, giving me a little nod. That's my sign. I take a deep breath and then lunge out from behind a tree. In a loud voice I call out the line I've rehearsed a dozen times.

"Stop right there, troll!"

Groo turns on me. His face twists into a convincingly horrifying sneer. He flexes his giant green arms and stomps his humongous green feet.

"Look what we have here!" Groo's gentle tone is gone, replaced by a rumbling growl. "A puny human!"

Groo plods toward me. The ground shakes beneath my feet.

"I'm gonna rip you apart limb from limb!" he yells. "Then I'll pulverize every bone in your body. And once that's done, I'll turn your brains into a stew!"

I cast a quick glance at our audience below. The farmer

and his wife are staring up at us, mouths hanging open in anticipation.

I summon up my loudest voice and yell my lines. "You've wreaked havoc on this land long enough! It's time to end your reign of terror."

Groo crouches like a wrestler about to enter the ring.

Our fight's about to start.

We go through the steps like a choreographed dance routine. He swings. I duck. He stomps in one direction. I spin in the other. His massive foot slams the ground in the spot where I was just standing. We have to be careful. One false step and Groo's fake death scene could become a *real* death scene for me.

His next punch comes a split second earlier than I'd expected. I scramble to dodge it just in time to avoid getting my teeth smashed in by his enormous green fist.

Groo pretends to lose his footing. As he stumbles, I rear back and throw my rock. It's supposed to hit him in the shoulder. But my aim's off. Instead, the rock pegs him right in the eye.

"Ouchie!"

All the intimidating bluster suddenly vanishes from Groo's voice. He rubs his sore eye like a little kid who's just been accidentally injured while playing peekaboo.

"That really hurt!" he whines.

"Sorry," I whisper. "Total accident."

Groo pouts for another second. Then he pulls himself together. Rising to his full height, he checks to make sure our audience is still watching (they are), and then bellows in his deepest, scariest voice.

"You'll pay for that, puny human!"

And that's when character number three joins our scene. Prince Fred. He steps out from behind a boulder, holding the flaming torch above him.

"Not so fast, foul troll!" He puffs out his chest, striking a hero pose. "Never again will you harm innocent humans or chickens. Prepare to die!"

Wielding his torch, Fred charges. Groo stumbles away from the flame. The chase leads all three of us behind a rock outcropping. While we're hidden from view, I clamber to the top of the rock. That's where I find our most important prop. The huge lump of moss that Groo carried down from his cave. It's been crudely shaped and tied together so that it appears to have a giant body. Two arms, two legs, a big round head.

A life-sized fake troll.

It looks nothing like Groo. But from a distance, we can only hope the farmer and his wife won't be able to tell.

Sewing thread has been tied around fake-Groo's mossy arms. I grab the piles of thread in my hands, then kick the lump of moss to the ground. By pulling the thread, I'm able to lift the fake troll off the ground until it seems to be standing on its own two feet.

It's sort of like putting on a big puppet show.

I swing the thread—left and right, left and right—creating the illusion that the troll puppet has just come lumbering out from behind the rocky outcropping. The real Groo keeps himself hidden, providing sound effects to match the action. A thunderous roar. An angry death threat. I pull at the thread so that the puppet's arms shake up and down as it "speaks."

Fred bolts out from the other side of the outcropping. He raises his torch and lunges at the fake troll. I yank at the thread, doing my best to make the lump of moss look threatening.

Fred jabs the puppet with his torch. Once, twice, three times. On the third attempt, the flame catches. Fire leaps and flickers against the green moss, quickly spreading from the puppet's stomach to its arms and legs.

From his hiding spot behind the rocks, Groo lets out a wail. "*RAAARRGGHHH! Noooo!*"

I swing the thread, causing the puppet to break into a

wild dance of pain. Orange flames blaze across its body. Before long, they burn through the thread and the puppet collapses into a fiery heap.

Groo stops screaming.

Groo is dead.

At least, that's what the farmer and his wife will think.

Hopefully.

Prince Fred

"You did it! You killed the troll!"

The farmer and his wife stare at us in awe.

"We're amazed you pulled it off," says the farmer.

His wife nods. "We thought fer sure you kids were gonna die."

"Gee, thanks," Kara mutters.

I stare at the slovenly pair of adults. Before today, I'd had a much higher opinion of humans than trolls. Now I'm starting to rethink all that. But at least the farmer and his wife keep their promise. They unlock the chicken coop, releasing Xyler from his captivity.

The cat leaps to the ground and scurries out of the stable. Kara and I quickly follow him.

On our way off the farm, we take a detour in the direction of the cow grazing in a field. When Gerta sees us, a clump of hay falls from her mouth.

"I can't believe what just happened!" she says.

"You shouldn't." Kara glances over her shoulder. When she's sure the farmer and his wife can't hear us, she turns back to Gerta. "It didn't happen."

"What do you mean?"

"We faked everything," I explain.

"Groo's perfectly safe," Kara says. "We staged his death."

The cow exhales a relieved breath. "Oh, thank the stars!"

"But you can't tell anyone. If any humans find out he's still alive—"

"Not to worry." Gerta gives us a steady look. "I can keep a secret."

Kara chuckles. "That's exactly what Groo said. He wanted us to thank you for not telling anyone what really happened to the chickens—"

"Including us," I say.

A smile hangs on Gerta's face, but there's a sadness in her eyes. This is goodbye. Each of us is aware of that. Although we haven't known the cow long, she helped us when we needed it. And now we're leaving. Forever.

I place my hand on her back, running my fingers through

her short brown hair. "Farewell, Gerta. Once our journey is through, perhaps we'll see each other again."

"Perhaps . . ." The word drifts in the air between us. It seems so small, so unlikely. But at least it's something.

After one last round of goodbyes, we turn and begin striding through the tall grass. Past the boundary to the farm. Along the way, I cast my gaze up the hill. Somewhere beyond my view is a cave. And inside is a troll, tending his hidden field of crops and chickens.

Groo. Another new friend we may never see again.

But for now, we have a quest to fulfill. With a sigh, I force myself to keep moving as that single word echoes in my mind.

Perhaps.

We spend the afternoon walking. Through rocky canyons and across rickety wooden bridges. Over rivers and between a steep range of hills. Our only guide is the Chasing Charm. The silver owl flaps through the air, its little metallic beak pointing us onward.

At a babbling stream, we stop for a drink. The water is frigid and delicious as it slides down my throat. Kara divides up a helping of the homemade bread and boiled eggs that Groo gave her before we left. Once we're finished with our meal, Kara and I rise to depart. Xyler doesn't.

"I can't go any farther," the cat complains between yawns. "It's been at least three hours since my last nap."

And so I pluck him off the ground. With Kara's help, I place him into the hood of my cloak. A cat-sized hammock, just right for Xyler to curl up and sleep in while we continue moving. He bumps softly against my back with each step.

But eventually, exhaustion catches up with me as well. I've never walked so far in my entire life. My feet feel as though they're filled with lead. But somehow I keep going. One heavy foot in front of the other. Trudging onward. Until a village appears in the distance.

I stumble to a stop, pointing at the buildings up ahead.

"It'll be dark soon." My voice comes out as a weak croak. "If we want to make camp somewhere, we should stop at that village for provisions."

Kara stares ahead, uncertainty straining at her features. "What if we're recognized?"

"We're a long way from the palace. I doubt these small-town folk have heard anything about my supposed abduction."

"And if they have?"

I gesture to our drab disguises. "Then they'll see two poor waifs in cheap rags. Just like the farmer and his wife did."

The look of doubt hangs in Kara's expression. "Seems risky."

"What other choice do we have?" I say softly. "We've almost run out of the food Groo gave us. And it gets cold at night. If we're going to be sleeping outside, we'll need blankets."

"Fine," Kara says. "Let's just try to avoid drawing too much attention."

"Agreed."

Kara points at my back. "That means no more cat hanging from your hood."

Xyler's muffled response comes from behind me. "But I was so comfortable."

"Too bad." Kara lifts Xyler out of his resting place and sets him on the ground. "I'm not sure about this town's pet policy."

"No need to worry." Xyler stretches. "We felines are masters at avoiding attention."

The village is little more than a few wooden shacks clustered around a dirt road. But at least there's a merchant's post. Kara and I push through the doorway and into the small shop.

A single lamp casts its flickering light across the shelves of merchandise. The selection is meager, but we manage to find what we're looking for. A bundle of blankets, a bag of apples, and a few links of dried sausage.

The shopkeeper behind the counter is a man with long dark hair. As we approach, he eyes us closely.

"You look like you're far from home," he says.

"Just passing through," I reply.

"That so?" He pushes back his dark hair. "And where might your parents be?"

I'd worried this question might come up, and I respond with words I prepared earlier. "We're orphans."

"Sorry to hear that," the man says in a not particularly sorry voice. "Heldstone can be cruel to parentless children. Especially in times like these. There are dark forces at work in the kingdom."

"What do you mean?"

"I've heard rumors of unrest in the palace. They say the king and queen have fallen ill. And that Grand Duke Sturmenburg holds the power until they recover." The man raises an eyebrow. "*If* they recover."

My heart sinks into my stomach. Even after everything that happened, I'd grasped tightly to a faint string of hope. But now it seems my worst fears are coming true. The poison is already taking effect. Mother and Father are dying. And treachery lurks inside the palace like a snake.

The shopkeeper leans forward. Long hair falls over his face like a curtain, but I can still feel his eyes drilling into me.

"And that's only the beginning," he says. "There are whispers that the grand duke has joined forces with a being of unspeakable power. A dark and magical being. They call her . . . the Shadow Queen."

The shopkeeper goes silent, but his words churn through my mind like a storm. *The Shadow Queen*. I have no doubt whom the name refers to. The Sorceress.

My heart pummels the inside of my chest. The more I try to control it, the louder it gets. By now, I'm sure every person in this village can hear it.

"Want to know the most troubling part?" the shopkeeper asks.

"Actually . . ." Kara plops our purchases on the counter. "Do you mind if we just buy this stuff and go?"

The shopkeeper continues speaking as if he didn't hear a word Kara said.

"People are claiming Prince Frederick has gone missing." The man peers at me through his dark hair. His head tilts slightly as his gaze moves to Kara. "He was abducted, they say. Taken by a girl about your age."

Wooden floorboards creak as I shift from one foot to

the other. A nervous voice rattles inside my brain. *Does he know?*

But then the man leans back and offers us an innocent shrug. And all of a sudden, the voice in my head fizzles away. He doesn't know. He's just a bored shopkeeper making conversation. Nothing more.

"Sorry for talking your ears off." He pushes back his hair. "Just thought a couple of orphans ought to know. Keep safe. As I said—dark forces stirring out there."

Back outside, Kara and I hurry along the dirt road with our newly purchased goods in our hands. Near the edge of the village, I cast one last glance backward. And there's the shopkeeper. He's standing in the doorway to his building. It's impossible to see his face behind his long black hair, but I'm sure of one thing.

He's watching us.

Kara

We hike into the woods, searching for a place to camp for the night. I listen to the sounds of twigs cracking and branches snapping. And something else. A faint rustling in the distance.

Grabbing Fred's hand, I come to a sudden halt.

He stops beside me. "What're you—"

"Shhh." I press my finger to my lips, listening. But now the rustling is gone.

Or maybe it was never there in the first place.

"I thought I heard something," I say.

"It was probably just Xyler," Fred replies. "He ran into the bushes a little while ago, looking for food."

"Yeah." I peer uncertainly into a tangle of bushes. "Maybe."

We keep going. Venturing deeper and deeper into the woods. But before long, I hear it again. Something stirring nearby. This time, Fred hears it, too. Whoever or whatever it is out there, it's a lot bigger than a cat. And it's getting closer.

Fred and I exchange a nervous glance. Without speaking a word, I can tell we both have the exact same idea.

Run!

In the next instant, we're dashing through the dense forest, weaving between trees and leaping over fallen branches. I'm sure I hear someone else out there crashing through the thicket, but in the commotion, it's impossible to know where any other sounds are coming from.

My momentum is suddenly shattered when a hand comes down on my shoulder.

"Gotcha!"

I whirl around to see the shopkeeper. A sword is clenched in his free hand. Behind his wild curtain of black hair, a smile lights up his face.

"I was hoping to run into you again," he says.

"Let me go!" I swing and kick, but the shopkeeper's grip only tightens.

A movement flashes in the corner of my eye. Fred rushing toward us. Xyler leaps from a branch above, baring his teeth. For a split second, I think the two of them might actually stand a chance against the shopkeeper. Then I feel something against my neck.

The cold, sharp sting of a blade.

Fred staggers to a stop. All the fight drains from his features, replaced by fear. Xyler slinks backward.

"Take another step and the girl loses her head." And just to make his point, the shopkeeper presses his sword even closer to my skin.

Fred holds up his empty hands in a gesture of surrender. "Please don't hurt her."

The shopkeeper aims a wily gaze in Fred's direction. "Back in the shop, I thought I recognized you. Now I'm certain of it. You're Prince Frederick."

"Nonsense." Fred's eyes drop to the ground. "I told you already. We're orphans. She's my sister."

"You don't look alike. You don't talk alike. If this lass is your sister, I'm an ogre's uncle. You're the prince all right. And this girl here." He gives my shoulder a painful squeeze. "She's the one who kidnapped you. There's a reward for your capture. Both of you."

Fred hesitates, thinking. "Very well, I confess. I *am* the

prince. Which makes my parents king and queen, remember? They'll double the reward. Triple it. Wealth beyond your imagining. All you have to do is release us."

"Your parents will soon be dead," the shopkeeper says. "They've already lost the throne to Grand Duke Sturmenburg and his Shadow Queen."

A chill grips my spine when I hear those words again. *Shadow Queen*. As if the Sorceress has already eliminated Fred's mother, as if she truly *is* the new queen. After seeing the kind of evil she could unleash in my world, I can only imagine the havoc she can wreak in Heldstone. Especially with the grand duke by her side and an entire army following her commands.

With such dark thoughts snaking through my mind, it takes a while for me to notice the sound. A rumbling in the air, as if a storm is coming. Almost like . . .

Thunder.

I glance up, but the night sky is clear and cloudless. No sign of rain.

And yet the thunder grows louder. A violent crashing that causes the ground to tremble and the trees to shake.

"Wha . . ." The shopkeeper swallows half the word in a fearful gulp. "What *is* that?"

Prince Fred and Xyler exchange an uncertain glance. They're obviously just as clueless.

Meanwhile, the thunder roars closer.

BOOM!

CRAAACK!

CRUNCH!

All of a sudden, a nearby tree collapses. Tangles of bushes and vines part like a curtain.

And that's when Groo makes his entrance.

I stare up in disbelief. I never thought I'd be so happy to see an enormous, terrifying troll.

Groo towers above our group, flexing his massive green biceps. I'm fully aware that he's a free-range-chicken-owning, homemade-bread-making, nature-loving, non-violent vegetarian. But it's easy to forget all that when I see him like *this*. Huge and horrifying. Stomping and raging and bellowing.

A total troll stereotype.

"RAAARRRRGGH!"

Still gripping me with one arm, the shopkeeper aims his sword at Groo. Big mistake. The troll snatches the blade out of his hands and snaps it over his knee like a twig.

"Next time, I break your spine!" he growls.

The shopkeeper staggers backward. "P-Please d-don't hurt me. I was just trying to . . . to help rescue Prince Frederick."

"Liar!" Fred aims an angry glare at the man. "All you cared about was getting a reward."

Groo grabs the man's collar between two massive fingers. Then he casts a glance at Fred and me, as if waiting for instructions on what to do next.

"Shall I rip *all* his limbs off?" he asks us politely. "Or just his arms?"

The shopkeeper lets out a whimpering sob as Groo reaches for his arm. I know it's an act, but the shopkeeper *doesn't*. It's obvious he'll do anything to protect himself.

Which gives me an idea.

"Wait!" My voice pierces the tense silence. "Let him keep his limbs. For now. But only under one condition."

"Wh-what is it?" the shopkeeper whimpers. "I'll do whatever you ask."

"Go straight to the nearest Royal Guard outpost and tell them we escaped."

Fred shoots me a confused glance. But there's no time to discuss our options. I give him a look that says, *Trust me.* Then I turn back to the shopkeeper.

"Next I want you to tell the Royal Guard that we're headed south," I say.

Realization flashes across Fred's features. He knows just as well as I do that we're *not* going south. The Chasing Charm has always led us west.

"That's right," he says, catching on. "Tell the Royal Guard we mentioned a destination in the Southlands. Tralbard. If they want to find us, that's where they should go."

Because we'll be nowhere near there.

The shopkeeper nods eagerly. "I shall tell them exactly that and nothing more."

"Good," I reply. "Because we know where you work. And if you don't keep your word, we'll send our troll friend to have a little talk with you."

Groo leans in close, snarling in the shopkeeper's face. "And next time I won't be so pleasant."

The second he's released, the shopkeeper turns and staggers away.

I turn a thankful gaze in Groo's direction. "You saved us!"

Groo shows off a toothy grin. "Happy to help!"

"But what're you doing all the way out *here?*" Fred asks. "We're nowhere near your cave."

"Yeah . . . about that." Groo scratches behind his ear,

suddenly awkward. "Here's the thing. Your visit reminded me how nice it is to be around others—especially when they're not trying to kill you. Once you left, I was all alone again. I mean, sure, I had my chickens. But they're not much for conversation. So I set out to find you. I figured maybe—y'know, if you'd be interested—well . . ."

"Let me guess." The hint of a smile forms on Fred's face. "You were hoping you could join our quest?"

"Because if so, that would be *awesome*!" I add.

Xyler nods enthusiastically. "A troll would be a terrific addition to our team."

"Really? Seriously?" Groo's excited glance bounces around our group. "Thank you so much, you guys!"

"You just saved our butts," I point out. "*We* should be thanking *you*."

＿

After camping for the night, our party (which now includes one very big new member) sets out bright and early the next morning. Following the flying owl necklace, we soon emerge from the forest and reach a stone-paved road. As we approach, I notice a crooked post at the edge of the path. A sign has been nailed to the wood, and it's flapping in the wind.

COME ONE AND ALL
TO MARVEL AT THE
STUPENDOUS &
FANTASTICAL
ELEKTRO-
MAGICIAN
A TRAVELER FROM THE
FAR-OFF WORLD OF URTH!
HE WILL FASCINATE
& AMAZE YOU WITH
SPECTACULAR STORIES
OF HIS ALIEN HOMELAND
AS WELL AS ASTONISHING
TRICKS OF MAGIC &
ENCHANTMENT
PERFORMING TWICE DAILY AT THE
RUINS OF GUIRWELDE
PRICE OF ADMISSIO
5c FOR ADULTS
3c FOR CHILDRF

Groo scratches his head. "Who's the Elektro-Magician?"

I stare at the sign as the ground drops out from under me. "He's my dad."

Prince Fred

I first heard of the Elektro-Magician only a few days ago—although looking back, it feels like many months. I was in the Royal Tutor's chambers when I noticed a slip of parchment. On the wrinkled, dirt-smudged page was a poem. The first few lines etched across my memory.

> *From a distant, unknown land came he*
> *A Traveler, he claimed to be*
> *People flocked, far and wide, to listen*
> *To the fantastical tales of the Elektro-Magician*

I stole the parchment and brought it with me to Urth. That's where I heard the Elektro-Magician's name uttered once again. Or . . . almost. The strange syllables came out differently when Kara said them:

Electrician.

Kara's father discovered the portal to my world while inspecting the broken walk-in refrigerator at Legendtopia.

That was three years ago. He's been here ever since.

After another hour of hiking, we gain our first glimpse of the Guirwelde ruins. A desolate landscape of charred stone—the only remains of a castle that was destroyed centuries ago.

And in the middle of these ruins, a massive carnival is taking place.

Mobs of people swarm between the crumbled walls, staggering in and out of open-air tents. Wild entertainment swirls all around them. Men on stilts juggling swords. Witches selling counterfeit potions. Dancing bears. Archery displays. Fire-breathers. Jousting. Singing. Dancing.

Kara peers at the celebrations from a distance. "What is all this?"

"The Thurphenwald tribes put on these carnivals," I explain. "They're nomads. Traveling the kingdom, organizing festivities wherever they go."

Kara shields her eyes from the sun, squinting. "Do you see my dad?"

I shake my head. "We're too far away."

"Then let's take a closer look."

Kara hides her hair behind her scarf. I pull my hood over my head. The last thing we want is to be recognized. Or to draw attention to ourselves. Which means we probably shouldn't show up with a gigantic, terrifying troll. And so Groo stays behind. So does Xyler. The cat's already curling up on the grass for his midday nap by the time Kara and I set off for the carnival.

As we enter the carnival, a wild scene unfolds around us. Slovenly adults scream and curse. Spilling their drinks, they crowd around a ring where an armored faun has been forced to fight a unicorn.

A man stalks through the cheering throng, collecting bets and taking money. He wears a buzzard skull over his head like a helmet. His right cheek is branded with a burn in the shape of an X.

Kara shudders at the sight of the man. "What's the deal with buzzard dude?"

"He wears the marks of a Thurphenwald tribesman."

"So he's one of the people running this whole show."

I nod. "And so is she."

Kara follows my glance to a similar-looking woman. Same buzzard skull, same X scar. She's standing at the edge of a crater that's been filled with murky water. Above her is a hand-painted sign that reads:

Meet the Mermaid

Adults: 2c Children: 1c

Inside the cramped crater, a miserable-looking mermaid swims in small circles through filthy water.

"An actual mermaid," Kara whispers in awe. "And it's being treated like . . . like trash. It's awful."

My gaze wanders over other sections of the carnival. A game of cards has turned into a shouting match. Accusations of cheating escalate into an all-out brawl. Nearby, a troll in rags is trapped in a rusty cage. A mob of men and women jostles the bars, shouting insults and throwing rotten vegetables at the troll.

And looming over all of it, scarred faces peer out greedily from beneath buzzard skulls.

A tribesman at the center of the ruins calls out in a harsh, raspy bellow. "Right this way to witness the Elektro-Magician!"

"My dad!" Kara breathes. "Come on!"

We hurry through the crowd. When we reach a wooden gate, a Thurphenwald woman glowers down at us.

"Six coppers," she grunts.

Kara digs through the purse where she keeps the money earned from my ring, removing a coin with two small holes punched through it.

She shows it to me. "Is that enough?"

"That's more than enough," I reply. "It's a twenty-copper piece."

Without hesitation, Kara offers the coin to the tribeswoman. "Here you go. Can I get change?"

The scarred woman laughs as she pockets the coin. Then she shoves us through the gate.

"Not the best customer service," Kara mutters. But there's no point arguing with the tribeswoman. It wouldn't be a Thurphenwald carnival if you didn't get cheated at least once. Besides, we have more important things to worry about.

Kara's father is somewhere up there.

We jostle our way through a forest of arms and legs. The audience numbers in the hundreds. It's impossible to see the stage through the thick swarm of other people. But everyone's facing in the same direction. And so we keep moving that way. Pushing forward, dodging elbows.

A crack in the crowd opens up. Kara and I dart through it.

And all of a sudden, we're in the front row. Ahead of us is a thick base of stone. And standing upon it is a single man. One glimpse of his face is enough to know . . .

He's Kara's father.

Kara

⁓

*D*ad.

The sight of him fills a hole inside me. A hole that opened up the day he vanished three years ago. Tears form a path down my cheeks. I swallow a sob, wiping the wetness from my cheeks.

It's him.

It's really him.

Dad's black hair hangs down to his shoulders. Much longer than it ever was before he vanished. New wrinkles have formed on his face. Across his forehead. Branching out from his brown eyes. A sadness clings to his features that was never there before.

He's wearing his old electrician's uniform. Blue coveralls with his name stitched into the chest. I guess in a place like Heldstone, the clothes seem exotic. Magical even.

He paces the stage, casting his gaze out into the crowd. He hasn't noticed me yet. And now I find myself wondering: *Will he even recognize me?* It's been three years. I'm older now. Taller. And I'm a long way from home.

When he speaks, another wave of feeling crashes over me. I thought I'd forgotten his voice. But hearing it now, it's as if no time has passed.

"Ladies and gentlemen, my name is Santiago Estrada. But you may call me the Elektro-Magician." Dad grew up in Argentina. His accent turns every word into a kind of music as he speaks his rehearsed lines. "I come from another world. A world known as Earth. A world with its own form of magic. The magic of *science*."

On a table beside him is a toolbox. It's the same toolbox he took to work with him every day. Dad opens the box and removes a series of objects. A circuit board. Colorful bundles of wires. A hand crank. Each one sends a jolt of recognition through my memory. He used to plop them down on the living room floor, showing them off for my brother and me.

His hands fluidly move across his instruments. Connecting wires, latching parts into place. As he works, he continues his speech.

"The magic of technology makes it possible for carriages to move without horses. It enables people to have a conversation from opposite ends of the world. On Earth, winged machines soar through the air and light can be cast without a flame."

Dad pulls another object out of his box. A lightbulb. After twisting a wire around the base, he begins turning a hand crank. Faster and faster and—

The bulb begins to glow.

The crowd lets out a collective gasp.

"This same magic is able to perform a lovely concert . . ." Dad raises an eyebrow. "Without a single musician."

He attaches his wires to a homemade speaker. I remember him building the speaker in our garage when I was in the second grade. As he turns the crank again, an electronic whir spills out of the speaker. With his other hand, Dad adjusts a set of knobs and dials. The sound shifts and changes, transforming into a soft melody.

A ripple of amazement passes through the audience. Hushed whispers, bewildered laughter.

Dad always put on a good show. Everyone around me is enraptured. But even as he grins and calls out his lines,

I can see the tug of sadness in his eyes. At either end of the stage, those Thurphenwald freaks are keeping a close eye on him. Glowering in his direction from beneath their creepy buzzard helmets.

"And for my next display of technological wonder, I would like to show you—"

Dad's voice staggers to a halt. For the first time since we arrived, his attention has landed on the front row. And now he's staring at one very specific member of the audience.

Me.

I wondered earlier whether he would recognize me after so long. Well, now I have zero doubt. All the color drains from his face. His eyes go huge with disbelief. And in that moment, the people in the crowd vanish. The creepy buzzard guys fade into nothing. Even Prince Fred ceases to exist. It's as if there's nobody else in the world.

Nobody but me and dad.

Dad and me.

Us.

Every muscle in my body wants to storm the stage. Rush into his arms. Bury my head in his chest. But that would be a bad idea. Dad's guards are already looking ticked off. His show just skidded to a stop and the Thurphenwald creeps obviously don't approve. One of them takes a menacing step toward him. The buzzard beak hangs low over the dude's scarred face. His hand inches toward his belt, wrapping around the hilt of a crooked dagger.

Before the guard can get any closer, Dad snaps back into performer mode.

"My apologies for the interruption," he bellows. "Sometimes the magic of Earth amazes even *me*."

Chuckles spread through the audience. The Thurphenwald guard backs away.

Dad gives me one last look. And even though I haven't seen or spoken to him in three years, I know exactly what his eyes are trying to tell me.

Come and find me after the show.

And then he continues with his performance.

After the show, we bribe a Thurphenwald tribeswoman for a little alone time with the Elektro-Magician. She leads us around the side of the stage, past a series of troubling signs—

NO VISITORS
BEYOND THIS POINT

UNAUTHORIZED ENTRY
MAY RESULT IN TORTURE

ALL TRESPASSERS
WILL BE BEHEADED

"Uh . . ." I glance around nervously. "Are you sure it's okay for us to be here?"

The tribeswoman only glares at me from below her buzzard helmet. Then she points a crooked dagger in the direction of a locked cage.

Dad is crouched inside.

I run to the cage. On the other side of the bars, Dad rushes forward. For several seconds, neither of us says a word. I can feel his eyes examining every detail of my face, as if comparing the girl in front of him with the daughter from his memory. The daughter he hasn't seen in three years.

"It's really you." His voice trembles. "I—I can't believe this."

I wipe away a tear. "Ditto."

His electrician's uniform looks two sizes too big. From up close, I can see how much skinnier he's become. His dingy cage is too small for him to stand at full height, and so he's hunched forward. But even in these miserable conditions, Dad looks overjoyed. He reaches for my hand, but freezes at a sound behind us. A harsh grunt from the tribeswoman. Above the X scar on her cheek, her eyes are pure malice.

"No touching," she warns.

Dad's hand slides backward reluctantly.

The Thurphenwald woman crosses her arms and takes a step closer to us. With her looming so close, I can't tell Dad any of the things I really want to say. How Mom and my brother, Neal, and I have never gone a day without thinking about him. The crazy quest that brought me here.

And we definitely can't discuss how I'm supposed to break him out of his cage.

If I don't want to raise any suspicions, I'll have to choose my words *very* carefully.

"I'm . . . uh—such a huge admirer of yours," I say. "My friend and I traveled such a long way to see you."

Dad stares in wonderment. "I can only imagine."

"My mother and brother couldn't . . . er—make the trip. They're back at home. But I'm sure they would love to see you someday. Somehow."

Dad nods with understanding. "I'd like that, too. Very much. Unfortunately, that might be . . . difficult." He squeezes the bars of his cage. "Under the circumstances."

"Maybe we can . . . find another way."

Dad's eyes gleam. "Maybe so."

Our conversation is interrupted by another rude grunt.

"Time's up," says the Thurphenwald tribeswoman.

I twist a desperate glance at the woman. "Please. Just a few more minutes."

She only shakes her head. "You've trespassed too long already. Now you leave."

I turn back to Dad. Stare deep into his eyes. When he speaks, his voice is full of hidden significance.

"I guess this is goodbye," he says. "For now. But as long as you're here, you should take a look around. This carnival can be so *distracting*."

The last word hangs in the air, thick as smoke. Before he can say anything else, the tribeswoman jabs me in the side with her boot.

"Let's go." The grip on her dagger tightens. "Now."

My head is crowded with questions, with things I still need to say, with the truth I'm not allowed to speak. Not here. Not with this sinister buzzard lady so close.

She shoves me. We begin walking.

Glancing backward, I manage to catch one last glimpse of my dad. Clinging to the bars of his cage, tears in his eyes. Suddenly, we turn a corner and he's gone.

Next thing I know, Fred and I are wandering through the carnival again. People all around us. Shouts, laughter, the smell of cooking food in the air.

"Well," Fred says. "What now?"

My gaze sweeps across the raucous scene all around me before finally landing on Fred. "Now we break my dad out of here."

Fred narrows his eyes at me. "Yes, but *how?*"

"Didn't you hear him?" The tiniest smile cracks my lips. "He told us exactly what we need to do."

Prince Fred

Has Kara lost her mind? She's acting as if her father just handed over instructions about breaking him loose. And yet—I was there. He said no such thing. Certainly not with the Thurphenwald tribeswoman hanging on their every word.

To make matters weirder, she now insists on touring the carnival, making extremely peculiar observations about her surroundings.

She points to a man blowing flames from a torch. "Do you think that fire-breather is afraid of horses?"

"Uh, I have no idea." I scratch my head. "Why?"

But by now, she's already on to another attraction. "See that fairy habitat?"

"Yes, but—"

"How heavy do you think it is?"

"I haven't the faintest clue."

She scratches her head. "I bet it's not too heavy."

"Too heavy for *what?*"

"I'll explain later." She turns her attention to another attraction: a huge wooden sign that reads THE MARVELS OF ALCHEMY. Pointing at the sign, she says, "Alchemy—that means they turn stuff into gold, right?"

"So they claim."

"Good. Let's go."

Kara hurries toward the exit. I stumble after her, my thoughts crowded with questions. It isn't until we find Groo and Xyler that she finally begins to explain.

"Okay, listen up," she says. "If everything goes right, these Thurphenwald punks won't notice my dad's missing until we're long gone."

"That sounds wonderful." I kick the ground with frustration. "But what in the seven moons is your *plan?*"

Kara reveals another slight smile as she gazes back at the carnival. "We're going to create the biggest distraction anyone here has ever seen."

Kara

Listen up, people! I'd like to present the Kara Estrada Guide to Creating a Massive Distraction and Rescuing the Elektro-Magician (aka, my dad):

STEP ONE: CREATE AN UNRULY MOB

See the alchemist over there? That's where we begin. Prince Fred and I gather in front of the wooden hut. And in voices that everyone nearby will hear, we yell in amazement.

"I can't believe it! The alchemist just gave me free gold!"

"Me too! This is incredible!"

"Free gold for everyone!"

The alchemist stumbles outside, bewildered. He attempts to claim that we're lying. But people don't hear him. They only have the attention span for two words:

"Free gold."

There is running and pushing. There are shouts and demands. It doesn't take long before an unruly mob forms.

STEP TWO: RELEASE THE FAIRIES

While a few dozen of those Thurphenwald jerks are busy dealing with the crazy scene outside the alchemist's hut, Groo sneaks over the fence. Ordinarily, people would notice the fifteen-foot-tall troll. But not now. Not while there's "free gold" to be had.

Groo makes his way to the fairy habitat. A huge box made of thick glass. It contains hundreds of miserable, trapped fairies. There's no way an ordinary human could push over the box. But Groo is neither "ordinary" nor "human." He shoves the habitat with all his strength. When it tips over, the top of the box breaks loose.

Fly away, fairies! You're free!

STEP THREE: FAIRIES + JOUSTING = EVEN MORE CHAOS

Here's the thing: the fairy habitat is located right next to a jousting tournament. Armored guys on horses who attack each other with long, pointy objects. A huge crowd is gathered to watch. After Groo liberates the fairies, many of them fly right into the middle of the jousting action. The horses completely freak out. They weren't expecting to be surrounded by a few hundred glowing winged creatures. They disobey the commands of the armored dudes and run madly into the carnival. All their riders can do is try not to fall.

STEP FOUR: WATCH OUT, FIRE-BREATHER!!!

Not far away, the fire-breather lifts a flaming torch to his face. He's about to do his thing when he notices a terrifying sight. A horse is barreling in his general direction. On top of the horse is an armored guy, his long, pointy lance swinging wildly from side to side. All around, people are running and screaming. The fire-breather screams, too. But remember the torch? Yep, it's right there in front of his face. And when the terrified howl escapes his lungs, an enormous wave of flames ripples through the air.

A nearby wooden stand catches fire. The inferno quickly spreads. Luckily, the people inside are already gone. Maybe they were drawn by the distant screams of "Free gold!" Or went to gawk at the escaped fairies. Or fled from the disarray of the jousting tournament. Either way, they are nowhere nearby as the flames rise high into the air.

With mayhem breaking loose everywhere, the Thurphenwald tribespeople have completely lost control of their carnival. They scramble to put out fires, to catch the jousting horses, to recapture the escaped fairies. They have no time to deal with two kids, an ogre, and a cat.

As we hurry through the chaos, Fred points to a nearby hole in the ground. The mermaid, trapped in her dirty pool. The crowd is gone, but the mermaid is unable to climb out.

Fred has to yell to be heard over the sounds of screaming all around.

I hesitate. We still have more distance to cover before we reach my dad.

"Come on, Kara!" Fred grabs my hand. "Your father's not the only one being held captive!"

Fred's right. We have to help the others, too. We can't leave them here to die.

Together, Fred and I scramble into the pit. Grabbing hold of the mermaid's hands, we drag her out of the pit. Her fin flaps with fear when she catches sight of the gigantic troll that greets her at the top.

"It's okay," Prince Fred assures her. "He's a friend."

The fear fades from the mermaid's face. She speaks in a soft, melodious voice. "There's a lake not far from here. If you help me to the exit, I can crawl from there."

Groo slings the mermaid over his shoulder and carries her to the edge of the carnival. By the time he returns, Xyler has appeared at our side. He has a silver key in his mouth.

Xyler drops the key at Fred's feet. "Look what I swiped off one of the guards. We can use it to rescue the other captives."

Through the crazy landscape of fire and mass chaos, we find others who have been enslaved by the Thurphenwald tribe. Fauns, unicorns, trolls. Unlocking their cages, one by one, sending them into freedom. Until, eventually, we reach the area behind the main stage.

"Kara!" My dad calls to me from behind iron bars. "You made it!"

STEP SIX: REUNION

The key twists inside the lock. The door opens. Dad tumbles out of his cage and into my arms. For a long moment, all we can do is laugh and cry and hug each other tightly.

Me and Dad.

Dad and me.

Us.

I don't ever want to let go. But we both know the pandemonium won't last forever. If we want to escape, this is our best shot. I reluctantly take a step back from Dad. For the first time, he seems to notice my companions. A boy my own age. A cat. And a gigantic troll.

"Uh . . . so these are my friends," I say to him. "I'll totally introduce them soon. But right now, we should probably run for our lives."

Prince Fred

We trek until the Thurphenwald carnival is nothing more than a pillar of smoke in the distance. Groo carries Mr. Estrada's box of tools and Urth technology on one huge, muscular shoulder. Xyler naps on the other. Beside them, Kara holds her father's hand tightly. Her voice accompanies our footsteps as she tells the story of how we found him. The necklace and the walk-in refrigerator. My trip to Urth and our battle with the Sorceress. When she reaches the part about Grand Duke Sturmenburg's betrayal, I stagger to a stop.

At last, Kara has found her father.

And I've lost my parents.

When the others notice I'm no longer hiking, they glance back in my direction. I twist away from them. I don't want anyone else to see the anguish in my face.

A moment later, Kara is at my side. She brings a gentle hand down on my shoulder. "It's not too late, Fred. We can still save your parents."

"How?" The word trembles as it leaves my lips. "Even if we *do* somehow make it back inside the palace, we have no cure for the poison. It's only a matter of time until my mother and father are dead."

"Maybe not." Kara's father has joined our conversation. "I know someone who may be able to help."

I peer up at him. "What do you mean?"

"On their way to the ruins, the Thurphenwald chieftain insisted that the entire caravan go out of its way to visit a village. A very specific village called Yyerit. Apparently, one of the chieftain's wives was ill, and Yyerit is home to an old blind woman named Desmelde."

Kara's head tilts. "Why would they care about an old blind lady?"

"Because Desmelde is the greatest healer in the entire kingdom."

Kara leaps forward, grabbing her father's arm excitedly. "That's great! Maybe the healer can make us an antidote!"

A flame of hope ignites inside me. "Do you know how to find the village of Yyerit?" I ask.

Mr. Estrada nods. "If we hurry, we'll get there by nightfall."

—

After hours of hiking along a winding tree-covered path, we reach the edge of a hill. Peering down, I'm met by a view of paradise. A green valley, glittering streams, meadows overlooked by ancient trees. And at the center of it all: a village.

"There it is." Mr. Estrada points. "Yyerit."

I approach the village with Kara and her father, while Groo and Xyler stay behind. Mr. Estrada leads us to a stone building at the edge of Yyerit. A sign above the door reads POTIONS, ELIXIRS & CURES. Near the entrance, two creatures are chained to a metal post. At over twice my height, they possess the wings of a bird, the scales of a lizard, and the head of a lion. Sharp teeth, huge claws, a spiked tail—they look deadly no matter what end you happen to be standing at.

When Kara sees them, she stops in her tracks. "Uh . . . what *are* those things?"

"Grimleks," I say. "I've read about them in books, but these are the first I've ever seen in real life."

"They look like something from my worst nightmare."

"Don't be silly." I take a step in their direction, holding out my hand for them to sniff. "Grimleks are noble and rare creatures. I'm sure they're perfectly— *WAHHH!*"

I stagger backward when the nearest grimlek lunges toward me. Letting out a savage roar, it snaps its lethal jaws. If it weren't chained to a post, the monster would've had my arm for dinner.

I clutch a hand to my throbbing chest. "Okay, you were right. Grimleks are the worst."

With the grimleks growling at us, we hurry inside.

The walls are lined with shelves containing glass bottles of many different shapes and sizes. Leaning closer, I inspect their labels. There are cures for seasickness, balms for burns, potions for insomnia. One small vial contains a faint green liquid. A sticker on the outside reads *Very Vomitous Expunging Elixir. Fast-Acting, Long-Lasting.*

"Welcome, guests. What do you seek?"

The creaky voice comes from the other end of the shop. I spin around to see an old woman. Small and hunched, white hair hanging down to her frail shoulders. A thousand wrinkles are etched into her pale face. She stares straight ahead with unseeing eyes the color of milk.

Mr. Estrada is the first to respond. "Are you Desmelde?"

"Over the years, many have called me by that name," she says mysteriously.

"We're looking for an antidote to a very rare poison. Malinwrought."

At the mention of the dark word, a change comes over the woman. Her blank eyes widen. She clasps her bony hands together to keep them from shaking.

"I'm very sorry, but it grows late. You should be going."

"Please!" I take a step toward the healer. "We need your help!"

Desmelde shakes her head. "I'm afraid there's nothing I can do. Now, I really must close the shop."

I exchange an uncertain glance with Kara and her father. What now?

Turning back to the healer, desperation clings to my voice. "We traveled a great distance through many dangers to be here. You're our last hope."

"You should think better than to place your hope in an old blind woman," she replies. "And if you don't depart this second, I'll send my grimleks after you."

I shudder at the memory of the winged, scale-covered, lion-headed monster. And yet—I cannot allow this woman to scare me off so easily. Out of desperation, I blurt out the only other thing I can think to say:

"My parents are the king and queen of Heldstone," I say. "Without your help, they'll die."

A curtain of silence falls over the room. Kara cuts me a worried look. The entire kingdom is searching for the Royal Prince. I'm supposed to be hiding my identity, not *announcing* it. We both know what'll happen if this woman shares what I just said.

We'll be dead before the day is done.

At least the healer is no longer insisting that we leave. Instead, she begins tottering toward me. A severe expression hangs on her wrinkled face. When she reaches me, she comes to a stop. Her eyes are pure white, and yet . . .

It's as though she can see me.

As though she can peer deep into my innermost self.

Kara

⁓

The healer stares at Prince Fred. Which doesn't make much sense considering she's blind. After a long moment of silence, her expression changes. Her white eyes widen. She nods once, as if making up her mind.

"Come this way," she says. Then she turns and slowly charts a path in the direction she came from. Toward a door at the back of the shop. Without looking back, she steps through the dark doorway.

And vanishes from view.

Prince Fred casts a baffled look my way. All I can do is shrug back at him. I have no idea whether we can trust this old lady—especially now that Fred has blabbed his true identity. But right now, we don't have any other choice.

Our group stumbles after Desmelde. Down a narrow hallway and into a dim stone room that looks to be the healer's workshop. On a table, there are a dozen clay bowls, each containing colorful combinations of herbs and crushed leaves. The shelves are stocked with ancient books. A cauldron burbles on the stove.

Desmelde points to a wooden bench. "Please, sit."

We do as she asks. In front of us, flames crackle inside a fireplace. For a long moment, Desmelde doesn't say a word. Simply peers into the flickering fire with her milky-white eyes. I'm beginning to wonder whether she expects one of us to break the silence when she finally begins to speak.

"In all my years as a healer, not once have I received an inquiry about Malinwrought. Until today. And would you like to hear the most peculiar thing?" The healer doesn't wait for our response. "You are the second visitors who have asked about Malinwrought in the past twelve hours."

Prince Fred leans forward on the bench. "Who were the first?"

"A regiment of soldiers," she says. "Working for Grand Duke Sturmenburg. Odd, wouldn't you say?"

The light of the fireplace glimmers across her features.

"I told them that Malinwrought went extinct centuries ago. So why would I need a cure? But the soldiers wouldn't accept my explanation. They insisted on searching my shop. I stepped aside. I told them to do as they wished."

"Did they find anything?" I ask.

The old woman shakes her head. "No. But I did."

"What do you mean? What did you find?"

"Answers." A slight smile forms on the healer's face. "While the soldiers inspected my shop, I listened. I heard heavy boots stomping the floor and large hands reaching into dark places. When I concentrated, I heard other things. Glimmers of their thoughts."

My grip on the bench tightens. Desmelde's voice mingles with the crackling of logs inside the fireplace.

"And inside the soldiers' thoughts," she continues, "I found lies. Betrayal. And fear. They were working for a power of unspeakable evil. A creature of pure darkness that sent terror through the soldiers."

I didn't need to read anyone's mind to know who the healer was referring to:

The Sorceress.

The Shadow Queen.

"This dark power ordered the soldiers to search for anything that can undo the effects of Malinwrought," says Desmelde. "And to destroy it."

"Wait, so ..." Fred's voice trembles. "You said they

didn't find anything. Does that mean . . . you don't have a cure?"

The healer's blank eyes reveal nothing. "That is what I told the soldiers. And it is what I was prepared to tell you. Then I listened to your thoughts. And I heard truth. You *are* Prince Frederick the Fourteenth."

The woman slowly navigates the crowded room with ease.

"I was saddened by the news of the king and queen's sudden illness," she says. "They're worthy rulers. Honorable and just. They do not deserve to play in the treacherous games of the grand duke and his Shadow Queen."

When she arrives at a bookshelf, she runs her fingers across the worn leather spines of books. Her hand stops suddenly. She traces a fingertip across the grooves of binding, the gold letters. She removes a book and opens it. From where I sit, I can see a hollow space has been carved into the pages.

Nestled inside is a glass vial.

Desmelde plucks the vial out of its hiding place and begins her slow, steady path back in our direction.

"Malinwrought is a cruel poison. I had hoped it truly *was* extinct. But I kept this anyway." She lifts the vial. Clear liquid swirls inside. "An antidote to the poison."

Beside me, Fred jumps up from the bench eagerly. "I owe you a great debt! How can I possibly repay you for this act of kindness?"

"Be a good prince," replies the healer. "And someday, a good king. Rule Heldstone with honor and virtue. That is all that I ask in return."

Prince Fred nods once seriously. "I will do as you ask. I promise."

Hope stirs inside me. I watch as the old woman holds out the vial. Fred reaches for it. But before he can take the vial, a sudden change comes over the room. Inside the fireplace, flames erupt into a bright blaze. I stagger back, shielding my face. The entire workshop seems to glow with an eerie light.

Shadows leap out from behind table legs and stacks of books. They stretch from corners and pool across the floor. Even though I'm standing so close to a roaring fire, a chill grips my body.

The shadows are coming together. Forming a human shape. The dark figure rises against the stone wall. Staring at the dark form, terror howls in my mind.

The Sorceress has found us.

Prince Fred

"Did you really think you could escape from me so easily?"

The Sorceress's voice echoes through my mind. Her dark silhouette stands flat against the stone wall. Although she has no eyes, I can feel her watching me. Although she has no mouth, I can sense her triumphant smile.

Beside me, Mr. Estrada turns to Kara. "You know this . . . *thing?*"

Kara nods gravely. "We've met once or twice."

"How . . . ?" I stare up at the shadow woman. "How did you find us?"

"I knew you would seek the cure for Malinwrought," the Sorceress replies. "Your final desperate attempt at saving the king and queen. And of course, if the antidote exists anywhere in the kingdom, it will be here, in the workshop of Heldstone's most talented healer. I sent soldiers to destroy the cure, but it appears you managed to hide it from them, didn't you, Desmelde?"

The healer's white eyes narrow. "You have no right to be here, Sorceress."

"Nobody knows me by that name anymore," replies the dark figure on the wall. "You may call me the Shadow Queen."

"I'll do no such thing," Desmelde spits back. "And you will *never* be the true queen of Heldstone."

The fireplace ignites with a furious blaze. The shadow grows, rising higher and higher, stretching across the entire wall and onto the ceiling. It's as if she's a dark giant, looming over us.

"You dare question my right to the throne? I am the most powerful wizardess who has ever lived! I have worked, studied, trained. I have *sacrificed*. I have done so much more than this spoiled little prince. And yet—for a thousand years, his family has claimed the crown as their birthright. No longer! I am undoing the injustice of their monarchy. I am taking what is rightfully mine."

I clench my hands over my ears, but it does nothing against the voice bellowing in my head.

The huge shadow seethes in front of us, above us, all around us. "There is nothing you can do to stop the inevitable. The king and queen will soon be dead. Grand Duke Sturmenburg and I will take their place. Together we will rule Heldstone!"

"*No!*" Despite the fear inside me, my tone comes out defiant, angry. "We're going to stop you!"

Behind the darkness of the Sorceress's face, I can sense her lips curling into a mocking grin. "Big words from such a little boy."

"At least he's *real!*" Kara shouts. "At least he's not some weird shadow freak!"

For a moment, the dark figure ripples with anger. Then the storm passes. The Sorceress strikes a confident pose. "You're already too late and you don't even know it."

I take a defensive stance, awaiting her attack.

"Oh, you needn't worry about me," the Sorceress says. "I have no intentions of harming you. I'm too far away for that. I merely came to chat. And to distract you."

"Distract us from what?"

The Sorceress turns her dark gaze to the healer. "Perhaps you should tell them, Desmelde. You're the one who hears everything. What do you hear now?"

What in the seven moons is the Sorceress talking about? I whirl to face the healer, and my confusion instantly turns to dread. The healer's blank eyes widen with fear.

"I hear hooves," she whispers. "Men on horseback."

"*Soldiers* on horseback," the Sorceress corrects her. "*My* soldiers. I just needed to keep you occupied long enough for them to reach you. And now they have."

The shadow hangs over us for another moment like a conquering general. Then the eerie illumination flickers away. The roaring fireplace returns to normal. The Sorceress vanishes.

And in the sudden silence, I hear exactly what Desmelde described.

Hooves.

The soldiers are getting closer.

Kara

"There isn't much time." Desmelde presses the vial into Prince Fred's hands. The Malinwrought cure. "You must keep this safe. No matter what else happens."

"I will." He carefully slides the vial into his cloak.

"And you." Desmelde turns her milky gaze in my direction. In her hands is another vial. This one contains a putrid greenish liquid. "Take this with you. In the future, you may need it."

My eyes land on the label. *Very Vomitous Expunging Elixir. Fast-Acting, Long-Lasting.*

The soldiers are nearly here. Our lives are in danger. The fate of the entire kingdom hangs in the balance. And she just handed me . . .

Puking potion?

But there's no time to ask any follow-up questions. We're already on the move. Down the hallway, into the shop. When we reach the door, we're met by Groo and Xyler. The two of them look frantic and out of breath.

"We ran here as quickly as we could," the troll pants.

"Had to warn you," wheezes the cat.

"Soldiers nearly here."

"Lots of them."

Groo points a massive green finger. By now, the sun has completely vanished behind the hills. But even in the darkness, I have no trouble spotting them. A dozen soldiers on horseback thundering in our direction. The light of seven moons gleams against their silver armor, reflecting off their swords and battle-axes.

Backing away from this sight, I nearly stumble into one of the grimleks we encountered on our way in. Fortunately, they're too busy snarling at the approaching soldiers to pay any attention to me.

But still. I'd rather keep my distance.

My dad turns to the healer. "Do you have any weapons?"

"Weapons will not help you now," she replies. "You must leave."

"But the soldiers—"

"Soldiers are the least of our concerns." Desmelde's features sharpen. "The Royal Palace is a nest of treason, and you are the only ones who can stop it. Defeat the grand duke. Destroy the Sorceress. Save the king and queen. That is what you must do."

"Come with us," Prince Fred says.

The healer shakes her head. "I've lived my entire life in this valley. I won't let a few soldiers force me to leave."

My ears fill with the rumble of the approaching horses. "We can't just abandon you."

"By staying here, you would abandon all of Heldstone." The healer's eyes are blank, but her tone is clear. She's not backing down. "You must go now. Before it's too late. Take the grimleks. They'll help you reach the palace."

"*Grimleks?*" Fred casts a fearful glance at the duo of monstrous creatures. Their sharp claws scrape at the ground. Their lion faces snarl. "Uh . . . thanks, but no thanks."

"I'm thinking we stand a better chance of fighting the soldiers than taking a ride on those things," I say.

Ignoring our warnings, Desmelde strides toward the grimleks. Terror leaps inside me, but the monsters don't attack. Instead, they greet her like tame pets. She holds out a thin, wrinkled hand. A whisper leaves her lips.

Strange syllables that are lost among the roar of the soldiers.

She stops speaking. She withdraws her hand. And when my gaze falls on the grimleks again, their faces have changed. The predatory gleam has vanished from their eyes. They're no longer growling. In the same instant, both their heads dip low, as if sending out a clear signal.

Climb aboard.

My dad takes a nervous step toward one of the beasts. When it remains in its submissive posture, he moves closer. Turning to me, he holds out his hand. "It's safe, *hija*. You can ride behind me."

I start toward him, then freeze. There's still a problem with our escape plan. Groo is way too big to ride the grimleks. The creatures would be crushed under the weight of a troll.

As if he can sense my thoughts, Groo hunches down to my level. "It's okay, Kara. I'm better off staying here."

"But—"

"There's no time for argument," Groo interrupts. "If you want to get back into the palace, you'll need to be sneaky. And let's face it. I'm not very good at being sneaky. I have other talents. Like strength."

To prove his point, the troll heaves me off the ground

like I weigh nothing at all. He sets me on the grimlek's back. Next he hands my dad his toolbox.

"Wanna know what else I'm good at?" Groo asks.

"What?"

"Beating up puny little soldiers."

He shows off a toothy grin, casting a glance toward the men on horses. Hooves pound the earth. They're nearly here.

I give Groo's massive shoulder a hug. "I hope we'll see each other again."

"Me too. Now hold tight to your dad. The flight may get bumpy."

I follow Groo's suggestion just in time. As I wrap my arms around Dad's waist, the grimlek lurches into the air. Wings flap on either side of us. Next thing I know, we're soaring upward. The other grimlek appears beside us. Fred grips the lion's mane; Xyler huddles between his arms.

Looking down, fear twists inside me. One of the soldiers is aiming a bow and arrow up at us. He pulls the bowstring and is about to fire when a massive green fist smacks him in the chest. The soldier flips backward off his horse. By the time he hits the ground, the guy's out cold.

Groo wasn't kidding about his talent for kicking soldier

butt. I just hope it's enough. The troll may be big, but he's also badly outnumbered. Six other soldiers have surrounded him, their swords raised. A few are preparing to take a swing when Desmelde reaches into her cloak and reveals a glass bottle. Removing the top, she tosses its contents at the soldiers' feet. Liquid splashes into the soil. An instant later, the ground opens up. Vines rise from the dirt, climbing up the soldiers' legs, snaking into their armor, yanking them backward.

Groo and Desmelde are still locked in battle when the grimleks veer around a hillside. I twist backward, hoping for one last glimpse of the troll and the healer, but the view's completely blocked. Looking into the night sky, the seven moons hanging above us, I make a wish for their safety.

Then I grip my dad tighter. We still have a long way to go until we arrive at the palace.

Prince Fred

For such a horrifying monster, the grimlek is surprisingly comfortable. I rest my head in its soft mane, listening to the steady flapping of feathered wings. Watching the landscape drift far beneath us, I feel suddenly overwhelmed by the monumental task that lies ahead of us. Our next steps are:

1) Sneak into the most heavily guarded building in Heldstone.
2) Find my parents without getting captured or killed.
3) Expose the grand duke as the treasonous weasel that he is.
4) Defeat the all-powerful shadow sorceress who's taken over my home.

It's going to be a very long night.

Whatever it is that Desmelde whispered to the grimleks, it must've included directions to the Royal Palace. Because after a few hours of flight, familiar tall turrets rise above the horizon. We're nearly home, but we still have a long way to go.

We land in a grove near the palace walls. In front of me, Xyler yawns and climbs out of the grimlek's mane. Close by, Kara hops to the ground. Her father hands down his box of tools.

"Wait here," Xyler says. "I have some friends inside who may be able to help."

And without any further explanation, he scurries into the darkness.

Ten minutes go by. Then twenty. Still no sign of Xyler.

Kara shoots me a nervous look. "You don't think he's been . . ." Her voice fades. In the silence, I hear the word she couldn't bring herself to speak.

Captured.

I shake my head. "Xyler knows that palace better than anyone in the kingdom. He's skilled when it comes to avoiding attention."

"Then where is he?" Kara asks.

"And who are these friends he mentioned?" adds Mr. Estrada.

I can only shrug. And as more time ticks away, my thoughts sink into a pool of worry and fear. Removing the glass vial from my cloak, I trace my thumb over its smooth surface. Clear liquid swirls inside. The cure. It won't do any good if my parents die before I reach them. I'm about to suggest we find another way into the palace when a sound disturbs the silence. A rustling in the underbrush. An instant later, Xyler appears.

"Thank the stars!" I rush forward to pet the cat's head. "Is everything all right?"

Rather than answering, Xyler motions toward the palace with his paw. "Follow me. We must hurry."

And just like that, he vanishes into the brush again. We scramble to follow him. Emerging from the trees, I'm grateful for the cover of night. Guards stand at attention atop the walls. I just hope it's too dark for any of them to see us.

Xyler leads us to the back of the palace. As we approach the wall, a head leans out the window. I flinch, certain we've been caught. Then I take a second glance at the figure above us.

It's a dog.

"Ooh, goody!" The dog speaks in the voice of a teenage boy. A not-particularly-bright teenage boy. "Mr. Prince is back! And he brought buddies! Do any of you like to play fetch?"

"Not now, Robbie!" Xyler replies sternly. "Do you have the rope?"

The dog—Robbie—nods eagerly. "It's a lot longer than my leash!"

"And did you tie it around the foot of the bed like I showed you?"

Robbie nods again. Slobber splashes against my shoulder.

"Excellent," Xyler says. "Toss it down."

Robbie disappears from the window, then returns a moment later with a rope in his mouth. When his jaws open, the rope tumbles down to us.

Mr. Estrada approaches the rope, then hesitates. "Are you sure we can trust this dog? What if there are guards waiting for us at the top?"

"Robbie may not be the smartest animal in the kingdom," Xyler says quietly. "And like others of his kind, he lacks the charm and grace that we felines possess. But I can assure you, he's trustworthy."

This explanation is enough for Mr. Estrada. He hunches down and loops the end of the rope under the handle of his toolbox.

"What're you doing?" I ask.

He ties the rope into a tight knot around the handle.

"This way, we can heave the box up to the window once we're all inside."

I feel a tingle of annoyance. "My parents could die tonight. Do we really need to worry about your *tools?*"

"It's not just tools," he replies patiently. "I've been in captivity for three years. This box was my only possession. My only way to fill the time. I would tinker, I would build, I would *invent*. If we want to stop the Shadow Queen, we may need these items."

I cast a skeptical glance at the rusted metal box. What can it possibly do against the Sorceress? But arguing this point would only slow us down, so I drop the subject. Once the box is securely tied, Mr. Estrada stands.

"I'll go first. Xyler, you can come with me. Once we're sure it's safe, you two follow." His eyes land on me. He brings a large hand to rest on my shoulder. "If anything happens to me inside, please make sure my daughter gets back to her home."

I straighten my posture, holding his gaze. "I will do everything I can. That's a promise."

"Thank you."

Mr. Estrada lifts Xyler onto his shoulder, then takes hold of the rope and begins to climb. When they reach the window, the two of them hop inside.

A second later, Mr. Estrada's head pokes out from above the sill. "All clear. Come on up."

Kara climbs to the window, and I follow her. Mr. Estrada tugs the rope, lifting the toolbox from below.

I glance at our surroundings. We appear to be inside one of the palace's many guest chambers.

"The king and queen are two floors up," Xyler states.

"Are they still alive?" I ask at once.

Xyler hesitates. As the silence stretches on, worry snakes inside me.

"Xyler . . . ?" I begin.

The cat sighs. "I don't know whether they're alive or not. I wasn't able to get into their room."

"I see." My gaze falls to the ground. "We have to get to that room. As soon as possible."

"It won't be easy," Xyler warns. "Sturmenburg's guards are positioned in every hall, every stairway. Not to mention the four stationed outside the king and queen's chambers. For their *protection*, according to the grand duke."

Kara lets out a sarcastic snort. "Yeah right."

"With so much security, how are we going to move around the palace without getting caught?" asks Mr. Estrada.

"That's where me and my buddies come in!" Robbie wags his tail excitedly. "We're gonna create a promotion!"

"*Commotion*," Xyler corrects. "You and a few other animals will create a *commotion*."

"Will that be enough?" I ask.

"Only one way to find out." Xyler turns to Robbie. "Are you ready?"

Robbie's ears perk up. He nods several times.

"You sure you're ready?"

Robbie jumps up and spins around in an eager circle. "Yes! Yes! Yes!"

"Excellent," the cat says. "Then go get 'em!"

"Ooh, goodie! It's promotion time!"

The dog races across the room as if someone just threw a bone. He paws the door open, bolts into the hall, then begins barking loudly. A few seconds later, we hear more barking from elsewhere in the palace. A harsh "Meeeooow!" comes from a floor below. Through the partly open door, I watch a flock of parakeets flap past.

It doesn't take long before the animal noises are joined by human shouts and clomping footsteps. The sounds of guards rushing away from their posts to deal with the chaos.

Xyler's eyes glow with urgency. "It's now or never."

Our group hurries across the dark room. The others follow me into the hall and toward the stairs. At the sound of approaching footsteps, we crouch behind a sofa. An armored guard comes clanking past, chasing after a yapping poodle.

On the move again. Up the stairs. But when we reach the third floor, I stagger to a halt.

Standing in front of me, dressed in a shimmering gown that matches her green eyes, is a most unwelcome sight.

Countess Francesca.

A haughty smile lights up her face. "Hello, Prince Frederick. So nice to see you again."

Kara

Her again.

Awesome.

In the background, dogs bark and cats yowl. The rest of the palace has other things to deal with. It's just us and the countess.

Her sharp gaze passes across our group. When it lands on me, her snotty smile gets even snottier.

"Look who it is." She fluffs out her perfect hair with a dainty hand. "The girl who poisoned the Royal Couple and kidnapped the prince—"

"That's not what happened." Prince Fred steps forward. "Grand Duke Sturmenburg—he's the one who poisoned my parents."

"Oh, I know *that*," Francesca replies matter-of-factly.

Fred blinks. "You do?"

"Of course." Francesca's eyes narrow at me. "There's no way that a common girl like *this* could pull off such a complicated plan."

Beside me, my dad tenses. "Who *is* this brat?"

Francesca ignores him. "I'm well aware of how badly the grand duke wants the throne. I know he'd do anything to gain power. And that includes poisoning the king and queen."

"Then you have to help us," Prince Fred pleads. "You could tell the world the truth."

"You're right. I *could*." Francesca examines her manicured nails. "But I don't think I will."

"W-Why not?"

"I'm not sure if you knew this, but Grand Duke Sturmenburg just *happens* to be my second cousin. He doesn't have any children of his own. Don't you see what that means, Prince Frederick? With your parents out of the way—"

"You're next in line for the throne." Fred's face has gone pale.

"Exactly." Francesca arches a well-plucked eyebrow. "And since you've made it perfectly clear you have no intention of marrying me, this is my best chance to become queen someday."

"Y-you can't do this, Francesca. You must listen to me. I'm still the Royal Prince—"

"Not for much longer."

Francesca looks like she's about to call for the guards, but she never gets the chance. Because while she's been talking, I've reached into my purse and removed a small glass vial. I uncap the top. And in the instant before the countess screams, I splash the contents of the vial into her open mouth.

"Gah." Francesca coughs. "What *was* that?"

I hold up the vial for her to view the label. *Very Vomitous Expunging Elixir. Fast-Acting, Long-Lasting.*

"You think that's going to stop me? Not a chance. I'm going to enjoy watching you die, you common little— GLURF."

Francesca makes a gagging sound. She quickly covers her mouth with a dainty hand.

"Is everything okay?" I ask in a tone that's somewhere between sweet and sarcastic. "You're not looking so hot."

That's an understatement. Within seconds, her face has turned a sickly shade of green. Her eyes bulge. She looks around, as if desperately searching the hallway for the nearest barf bag.

My memory bounces back to what Desmelde the healer

said to me as she pressed the vial into my hands. *Take this with you. In the future, you may need it.*

I'd had no idea how right she was.

Francesca bolts down the hall and into the nearest doorway. A moment after the door slams shut, we hear the muffled sounds of . . .

Well, you can probably guess.

I drop the empty vial back into my purse. "That ought to keep her busy for a while."

Our group spins around the third-floor landing and continues up the stairs. When we reach the fourth floor, Xyler points down a long corridor.

"The king and queen are that way," says the cat. "Even with the distraction, the way there is sure to be heavily guarded."

"It won't be easy to sneak around with so many people," Dad observes.

Fred nods. "Perhaps we should split up. Xyler and I will go the rest of the way on our own."

My worried glance passes from Xyler to Fred. "But what if someone spots you? If we're not there, we won't be able to back you up."

"Prince Frederick and I have spent our entire lives exploring this palace," Xyler replies. "We know it like the back of my paw. I can assure you—we'll remain unseen."

Prince Fred points to an open doorway. "Wait here. We'll be back soon."

Dad and I follow him through the door and into what looks like a medieval conference room. At the center is a long stone table surrounded by uncomfortable-looking chairs. Portraits of grumpy old men gaze coldly from gold frames. I flinch when I notice a suit of armor in the corner gripping a sword in its gloved hands. In the next moment, I realize—the armor's empty.

I turn back to Fred. "Just be careful, okay. I mean it. You're one of my best friends. In either of our worlds. If something happens to you . . ."

My eyes fall to the ground. A second later, I feel Fred's arms wrap around me. He hugs me close.

"Worry not, Kara," he whispers. "We shall see each other again."

I hope he's right.

Before I know it, Fred and Xyler are at the doorway again. They step into the hall, closing the door behind them.

Gone.

I look to my dad. "Okay, so . . . now what?"

He sets his rusted toolbox on the stone table and un-latches the lid. "Now we prepare."

Prince Fred

Xyler leads a zigzagging path through the palace. In and out of unoccupied rooms. Along the secret passageways used by servants. A tour through parts of my home that I didn't know existed. Emerging from a fireplace that turns out to be a hidden door, the cat points down the hall.

"Your parents are that way," he whispers.

We sneak closer. Turning a corner, I spot four guards standing outside a closed door. I take cover behind a marble statue, peering at the insignia on the men's armor.

"That's the grand duke's sigil." My jaw clenches. "They'll never let me through."

"Then you'll have to find another way past," Xyler says. "Wait here until the right moment."

And then the cat steps into the hallway. He casually struts in the direction of the guards, tail weaving in the air.

The nearest guard points with his spear. "There's the cat! The one the grand duke warned us about!"

"Get him!" yells another.

A third guard swings his spear, but Xyler's already on the move. The blade only makes contact with the floor. The rest of the guards scramble to catch the cat. Lunging, diving, grabbing. Throughout the chaos, I catch glimpses of Xyler. A fuzzy blur darting between their legs and behind their backs, just out of reach.

With all the clanging and shouting and chasing, none of the guards notice me opening the door to my parents' chamber and slipping inside.

The door clicks closed behind me. As soon as I whirl around, I see them. My parents. Lying side by side in bed. I rush toward them. But as I get nearer, an icy sliver of dread forms inside my chest. All the color has drained from my parents' faces. Their lips are pale blue. I grab my mother's hand, but her fingers are limp and cold.

They're already dead.

I'm too late.

A tear slides down my cheek. I did everything I could, but it still wasn't enough.

I reach into my cloak and remove the vial of

Malinwrought antidote. My movements feel discon-nected. As if I'm watching myself from a distance. Leaning over my father's pale face, I open his mouth. Just enough to pour half of the vial down his throat.

I know it won't make a difference, but I do it anyway.

I give the other half to my mother. I look down at them—their bodies as still as statues. Anguish rips my mind apart. I fall to my knees, pressing my head into my mother's unmoving arms. A cracked sob escapes my lungs. I don't care if the guards hear me. It doesn't matter. Noth-ing matters now that my parents are—

"*Son.*"

Through the storm of my grief, I hear it. A voice. At first, I'm sure it was just in my head. But there it is again. This time, slightly louder. Slightly clearer.

"Son."

I look up. When I wipe the tears from my eyes, I see my father peering back at me. Color is already returning to his face. Beside him, Mother stirs. Her eyelids flutter open.

She speaks in a feeble whisper. "We've missed you."

"I missed you, too." Wrapping my arms around my parents, it's as though I can feel the life returning to their bodies.

I want to apologize for leaving without telling them the truth. But I don't get the chance.

Because that's when a new voice shatters the moment into a thousand jagged shards. "I apologize for interrupting such a lovely reunion."

I spin around to see Grand Duke Sturmenburg staring down at me. His long fingers curl around the diamond-studded hilt of his dagger. *Shikkk.* The sharp blade slides out of its sheath.

"Would you like to hear something funny?" the grand duke asks. "When I was forming my plan to seize power, you were the least of my concerns. I mean, *really*—what was there to worry about? A spoiled little prince who's lived his entire life inside a great big palace? I could never imagine that *you*—of all people—would put up much of a fight. And yet . . . here we are."

Sturmenburg's grip on his dagger tightens.

"I'm going to do what I should've done days ago," he hisses. "Soon the kingdom will receive the tragic news. Prince Frederick is dead. And so are his parents."

"Y-you can't," I stammer.

The grand duke arches an eyebrow. "Ah, but I *can.* Quite easily. Your disappearance, the poisoning of the king and queen—it's all been blamed on the rebel girl. The one who seems to have appeared out of nowhere. Almost as if she's not from this world."

Kara. As Sturmenburg talks about her, his eyes narrow at me.

"I know the truth about your friend." His lips curl into a smile. "The Shadow Queen told me all about your adventure on Urth. And the girl you brought back with you. It's quite a story. How unfortunate that nobody else will ever know about it. The only version of events that matters is the one *I* tell. About how the rebel girl abducted the prince. And when he tried to escape, she murdered him."

The grand duke raises his dagger. Torchlight traces the diamonds and slides along the edge of the blade.

I cast a trembling glance over my shoulder. My parents. Still lying in bed, still weak from the poison. They can barely lift their heads. They won't be able to protect me. Or themselves.

The grand duke follows my gaze. "What a miraculous recovery! The king and queen—awake again! Although, I have a sneaking suspicion it won't last."

"You'll pay for what you've done." Father raises an arm, reaching for the dagger, but Sturmenburg easily knocks his hand away.

"I'm afraid you're quite wrong," says the grand duke.

"I'll be *rewarded* for my efforts. At last, the Kingdom of Heldstone will be mine."

In a violent burst, Sturmenburg lunges at me. I twist sideways—but not quite quickly enough. His blade grazes my arm. A flash of pain. As I scramble away, a crimson trail of blood follows me across the room. The grand duke catches up with me a second later. Grabbing my collar, he yanks me backward.

I see his dagger—a terrible glint of steel aimed at my chest. But before he can attack, I jam an elbow into Sturmenburg's midsection.

"*OOOF!*" He doubles over.

Instantly, I'm on the move again. Racing toward the door. I have to alert the rest of the palace, let them know the truth. The king and queen are alive. Grand Duke Sturmenburg is a traitor.

Everything's a blur. I'm running with all my strength. Almost there, almost there, almost—

The grand duke tackles me from behind. The ground rushes up and collides with me. All the air's knocked out of my lungs. I can't breathe. The cut on my arm throbs. But these are the least of my problems. Because when I turn onto my back, I'm met by a horrible sight.

Sturmenburg.

I thrash and swing, but he's too big, too strong. His knees pin me to the ground.

"After a thousand years, your family's reign is over." The grand duke raises the dagger above his head. "At last, a glorious new era shall begin."

My father's voice comes from behind him. "I wouldn't be so sure about that."

Bewilderment splashes across Sturmenburg's features. Twisting around, he sees my father. Nightdress flowing around his ankles, three days' growth of beard on his face. But very much alive—and standing right behind the grand duke. Father holds a flagpole over his shoulder like a spear. And before the grand duke can respond, he swings.

THWACK!

The flagpole knocks Sturmenburg sideways. The diamond-studded dagger skates across the floor. I scramble to my feet and grab it. Then I rush to Father's side. He still looks wobbly on his feet. I sling an arm around his waist to keep him from falling.

Peering up at him, I feel gratitude swell inside me. "You saved my life."

Father's eyes gleam. "You saved mine first."

A weak groan comes from the floor. The grand duke is struggling to his knees.

"That'll be far enough," Father says.

And just in case his warning isn't enough, I hold Sturmenburg's dagger ready.

The grand duke glares up at us with wounded anger. "Kill me now and get it over with!"

"As much as I would like that, I won't grant your wish," Father replies. "You shall stand trial. All of Heldstone will know what happens to traitors and bear witness to your treachery."

Sturmenburg's lips twist into a strange smile. "You have not seen the full extent of my treachery."

With lightning-quick movements, his hand darts into his boot. A heartbeat later, it emerges again—gripping a small silver blade. Before I can respond, the grand duke springs forward, knife aimed at Father's stomach. At the exact same moment, a blur shifts in the corner of my vision.

Mother.

She heaves an antique vase above her head and—

CRAAASH!

And just like that, Sturmenburg's assassination attempt is thwarted by a flowerpot.

The grand duke collapses into a pile of shattered porcelain. Out cold. I rush to Mother's side, flinging my arms around her.

"I love you, son," she says.

Even though she's still frail from the Malinwrought, Mother holds me tight. Father joins her, enveloping us both in his embrace. After everything the three of us have been through, I wish the moment could last forever, but it can't. Not while a grave and terrible evil still lurks in the palace.

Taking a step back, I turn my gaze up to my parents. "We have to move quickly. Kara and her father are in danger."

Kara

⁓

I have no idea what my dad's up to, but it looks complicated. His supplies are scattered all around the stone conference table. Lightbulbs, batteries, tangles of wire. Other objects are scavenged from the room. He yanks a mirror off the wall and steals a sword from the suit of armor in the corner. It's half shop class, half fairy tale junk sale.

"Hey, *hija?*" Glancing up from the circuit board that he's fiddling with, he points a screwdriver. "See that telescope?"

"Yeah?"

"Could you grab it for me?"

"Planning on some stargazing?"

"Actually, I was hoping to remove a few of its refracting lenses."

I lift the telescope over my shoulder and carry it in Dad's direction. "Could you at least tell me what you're working on?"

"Like I said, I'm preparing."

"Preparing for *what*?"

Dad's expression darkens. "For the Sorceress."

A chill prickles my skin. As I look around the room, every shadow seems to pulse with possible danger. The Sorceress could be anywhere. And I honestly don't see how all this random stuff is going to help us fight her.

But at least this mystery project provides a tiny bit of distraction from our current situation. Like the fact that Prince Fred and Xyler have been gone for way too long. With every minute that goes by, I worry about them more and more.

Dad continues his work. Disassembling the telescope and using its parts for his invention. A weird mash-up of scraps and technology and random junk—some from his toolbox, others from the room.

I stare at what he's done so far. There are lightbulbs hooked up to a homemade battery. A box lined with mirrors and lenses. A sword wrapped in copper wire.

A half hour later, his work is interrupted by distant sounds from the hallway. I take a few steps toward the door, concentrating. I can hear the noise slightly better now. The echo of voices screaming.

"Do you hear that?" I ask.

Dad glances up from his work. He looks at me like someone who just came out of a deep dream.

The howling is growing louder.

"What is it?" he asks.

"I don't know. Whoever it is, it sounds like they're getting closer."

Just to be safe, I start looking around for possible weapons. A screwdriver and a hammer. Holding one in each hand, I look like I'm about to build a birdhouse, not fight an evil army.

As the parade of echoing noises approaches, I begin to recognize some of the words they're yelling.

"Rejoice! Prince Frederick is back!"

"The king and queen—they're alive!"

"The grand duke is a traitor!"

The fear inside me dwindles away, instantly replaced by relief. The mob outside isn't angry. They're celebrating.

All of a sudden, the door flings open. In marches Prince Fred, looking like he's just been in a fight. His clothes are rumpled and torn, stained with bright splashes of blood.

I rush toward him. "Are you injured? What happened?"

He casts a glance at the bloody gash in his sleeve as if he'd forgotten it was there. "Oh, *this*? The grand duke stabbed me."

"*Stabbed* you? Is everything okay?"

"I'm perfectly fine. Nothing but a minor cut."

My voice spills out quickly, edged with worry. "Are you sure? It doesn't *look* minor. There's blood everywhere. And what about Sturmenburg?"

"He's been captured."

Behind Fred, two other figures have appeared in the doorway. The king and queen. Dressed in flowing nightgowns, they navigate a slow path in our direction.

"This must be Kara." The queen smiles down at me. "Our son speaks very highly of you."

The king brings an arm to rest on his wife's shoulders. "Frederick has told us what you've done to protect this kingdom from treachery. And to save our lives."

The queen's eyes rise above my shoulder. "And this must be your father."

Bowing deeply, Dad's voice is weighted with respect. "It is a great honor to meet you both."

With the flick of her hand, the queen lets Dad know he can stand. "The honor is all ours."

"Is it true what we've heard?" The king's eyes widen with enthusiasm. "Are you really the man known as the Elektro-Magician?"

"I've been known by that name for the past three years. But thanks to these two"—Dad's eyes pass from me to Fred—"I can finally go back to my old life."

"On Urth?" the king asks excitedly.

Dad nods. "Yes, Your Majesty."

"How enchanting!" The queen shows off a radiant smile. "I'm sure you're eager to return to your home."

Prince Fred and I exchange a glance. Our parents actually seem to be getting along.

Too bad the nice moment ends so quickly.

Out of nowhere, the conference room door slams shut. An ominous echo rings through the sudden silence. A guard at the edge of the room grabs the door handle and pulls as hard as he can.

It won't budge.

He turns his bewildered gaze toward the king and queen. "It's locked!"

Staring into Fred's eyes, I can tell he knows exactly who's responsible for what just happened. And so do I.

Just in case there was any doubt, the atmosphere of the room suddenly shifts. Like a storm moving in, a chill spreads through the air. The torches that line the wall flicker and hiss. Darkness dances against the wall and pools in the center of the floor.

All our group can do is stand there, frozen with fear, watching as the shadows take shape.

Prince Fred

I never thought I'd say this, but I miss the Sorceress. The old Sorceress. The one who existed before she transformed herself into *this*—

The Shadow Queen.

Sure, that old Sorceress turned Kara's town into a fantasy wasteland. And yeah, she made several attempts to kill or capture us both. But she was never as terrifying as she is now. A figure of pure darkness stalking across the room. Absolute evil lurks inside her inky-black form.

"Stop at once!"

The guard clenches his spear and charges the Shadow Queen. Bad idea. She flicks a hand toward the guard, casually, like brushing away an insect. An invisible spell pulses from her fingertips. In the next instant, the guard stops running. The spear drops from his hands. He crumples to the ground. He doesn't move again.

My trembling glance passes across the rest of our group. Kara. Her father. My parents. And Xyler. We have the Shadow Queen outnumbered, but I doubt that'll help. Not when she's vastly more powerful than us.

There's a pounding at the door. The crowd in the hallway doing everything they can to get inside. It's no use. The Shadow Queen's magic holds the door firm.

There's no way in.

And no way out.

"Did you really think you could escape me?" The Shadow Queen's voice booms against the walls of my skull. "From the moment you returned to the palace, I've been watching. You can't run from the shadows. They're everywhere. *I* am everywhere."

Her dark, featureless gaze turns to me. I feel my knees weaken.

"Prince Frederick," she says. "I watched as you snuck into your parents' chamber. As you brought them back to life. As you defeated Grand Duke Sturmenburg. And I *let* it happen."

I shake my head in disbelief. "Why?"

"Because I no longer *need* the grand duke. He served his purpose. He did my bidding while I gained strength. But I never intended to share the throne with him. Or anyone. Soon I—and I alone—shall rule Heldstone."

My father steps in front of me, shielding me from the Shadow Queen. "The people of Heldstone will never accept you as their queen!"

"The people of Heldstone will have no choice!"

The Shadow Queen points at my father. An invisible force heaves him off the floor and tosses him across the room. He lands in a heap on the floor.

"Evil witch!" Mother yells. "You shall pay for—"

In the blink of an eye, the Shadow Queen extends her arm. Mother's voice ends in a strangled gasp as a dark hand closes over her throat.

"*Stop!*" My own horrified scream echoes across the room. I thought I'd witnessed my parents die once today. Seeing it a second time is unbearable. "Let her go! I'll do whatever you want!"

Without releasing her grip, the Shadow Queen turns to me. "Is that so?"

I nod. "Please, just don't hurt her."

The dark figure gives this a moment's thought. And

then opens her shadowy hand. Mother collapses to the ground, gasping for air.

"Very well. Allow me to tell you what I want." The Shadow Queen sweeps toward me as she speaks. "I want to keep you alive long enough for you to watch your parents suffer before they take their last breath. Then, and *only* then, I will kill you. And as for your friend . . ."

The dark gaze shifts to Kara.

"This is what I want from you, little girl. I want you to take me to the door. The door to Urth. And before I put an end to your insignificant little life, you will see me begin my conquest of your world."

Even with the dark figure towering over her, Kara clenches her hands in defiant fists. "I'll never help you."

"Of course you will," replies the Shadow Queen. "Because that's the only way I'll let your father live."

The boldness fades from Kara's face. She whirls to face her father, who is standing beside a stone table that's covered with all manner of tools and equipment. His hand is resting on a strange box that looks as if it has been patched together from scrap metal. A telescope pokes out of one end like the barrel of a cannon.

"Don't listen to her, *hija*." Mr. Estrada grips the box tighter. "She'll never succeed."

The Shadow Queen lets out a mocking laugh. "Of course I will. My power is unsurpassed. I told you already: The shadow is everywhere. Nothing can stop it."

"Except the light," says Mr. Estrada. With these words, he flicks a switch beside the box.

All of a sudden, his strange invention begins to glow.

Kara

⌒

So that's what Dad's been working on all this time. The world's strongest flashlight.

From the telescope's lens, a beam of light blasts across the room. It's more powerful than anything I've ever seen. All the items he added to the box—lightbulbs, homemade batteries, mirrors—are channeled through the telescope. The result is a solid ray of illumination that shoots out of his box like a missile.

And hits the Shadow Queen right in the chest.

"RAAAARGH!"

The Shadow Queen lets out a howl of pain. She lurches away from the beam, but Dad's response is immediate. He swivels the box, keeping the dark figure in his spotlight.

No matter where she goes, the illumination follows her. The floor, the wall, the ceiling.

The shadow curls in agony. Her head twists in Dad's direction. Her pleading wail rips across the room. "*MAKE IT STOP! PLEAAAASE! JUST PUT AN END TO THIS CRUEL MAGIC!*"

"It's not magic." Dad's jaw clenches. His grip on the steel box is firm. "It's science."

"*I CAN GIIIIVE YOU SOOOOO MUCH MOOOOORE!*" As the shadow writhes, her pleading voice distorts, each syllable stretching until it's on the verge of being ripped apart. "*YOUUUU CAAAAAN RUUULE HELLLLDSTONE ANNNNND UUUUURTH!*" A flicker passes across Dad's features. And in that moment, I catch a glimpse of something inside him. The others may not have noticed, but I'm his daughter. I can tell.

There's some part of him that's actually considering her offer.

A shock runs through me. But in a way, it shouldn't come as a complete surprise. Dad's always had an oversized ambition. This is the same guy who moved to another continent, who started a new life in a new culture. Three years ago, when he discovered the miniature doorway, the portal to Heldstone, he took that risk, too. He ventured into a completely different world.

Now he has the opportunity to grasp ultimate power.

I take an unsteady step toward him. "Dad?"

At the sound of my voice, he turns to me. All at once, his expression changes. He shakes away the temptation.

But in the half second of distraction, the Shadow Queen jolts free from the light's beam. One dark arm reaches for me. I stagger backward. My vision fills with a pitch-black hand. I can feel the evil magic seeping into me. My eyes, my mouth, my skin. Crawling into my lungs, wrapping around my bones.

My insides turn to ice.

Everything goes numb.

My heart stops.

Falling and falling and falling and . . .

And a blinding light pierces the Shadow Queen.

And she releases her grip.

And life blinks back on inside me.

Breath suddenly fills my lungs again. I hit the floor, gasping for air.

When I open my eyes again, I see the shadow pinned into a corner. Dad lifts his invention off the table. The momentary flash of uncertainty has vanished. Now his resolve is firm. He carries the box forward. One step at a time. Closer and closer. The light drills into the twisted form of darkness. The shadow barely even resembles a human any longer. More like a dark mass of screaming and thrashing. A shriveled arm. A shrinking body. A withered head.

The Shadow Queen's wails fade.

When he's directly in front of her, Dad comes to a stop. The illumination burns through the final remnants of darkness. Until the shadow vanishes. Completely gone. At last, the Sorceress is dead.

Prince Fred

A month passes.

The Sorceress is gone. Grand Duke Sturmenburg is locked away in a heavily guarded prison cell, awaiting trial for treason. Life in the Royal Palace is returning to normal.

Or . . . almost normal.

There *have* been a few changes around here. These days, Mother and Father allow me to practice my swordsmanship with the knights—as long as I finish my lessons with the Royal Tutor first. Also, they're much more likely to listen to my ideas. Like my recommendation for Countess Francesca. She has been officially appointed diplomat to Stonk. For the next several years, she'll be living in the most remote corner of the kingdom, far from her snotty friends—and me.

That's not the only change. The Royal Palace has also gained one very big (and very green) new resident.

"Groo!"

My voice echoes across the courtyard, where the troll is tending his garden. Chickens roam freely through the rows of seedlings that have just sprouted. Groo smiles up at me.

"Your Highness!" he calls out. "Thanks again for letting me move here."

I jog toward him. "Of course. I'm just glad you were willing to leave the cave."

Groo shrugs. "Well, I *did* put a lot of work into the place. But then the farmer and his wife found out I'm not really dead. They wouldn't leave me alone. Villagers kept showing up with sharp pointy things and hard clobbering things and flaming hot things. It got annoying."

"Sounds like it."

"Plus, now I have lots more space for my organic garden!" The troll's eyes gleam with pride.

"Moo."

Our conversation is joined by someone else. A cow that just poked her head out of the stable.

"Gerta?" I stare at the cow in astonishment. "What're you doing here?"

She flicks her long eyelashes. "I live here."

"Really? That's wonderful. But ... why didn't anyone tell me?"

"Your parents wanted it to be a surprise. After Groo told them about what happened at the farmhouse, they insisted on bringing me here."

I wrap my arms around Gerta's furry midsection. She gives my ear an appreciative lick.

"Gerta's cheese really is the best," Groo says. "Plus, she can help me plan my free-range chicken habitat!"

"I'm so glad you're here." My gaze shifts from the cow to the troll. "Both of you. We'll have to chat more soon. But at the moment, I'm late for a meeting."

Waving goodbye, I jog the rest of the way across the courtyard. Throwing open the palace doors, I enter an opulent hallway. Around the next corner is the Hall of Kings.

The walls are lined with gold-framed portraits of my ancestors. Those who came before me, those who share my name. Men remembered by history for their bravery and honor. There is King Frederick the Fierce, thrusting a sword as he leads an army into battle. And King Frederick the Giant Killer, facing down a monstrous creature that towers above him. And of course, my great-great-great-great-great-great-great-great-great-great-grandfather, better known as King Frederick the Bold. In his portrait, he's wrestling a bear, just for the fun of it.

"Ah, Frederick! Just in time!"

Mother waves to me from across the room. Father stands beside her, an arm wrapped around her slender waist.

"We were just about to unveil the newest portrait," he says.

"Can we make it quick?" I ask. "Don't forget, we have that meeting soon."

"Of course," Mother replies. "But we think you'll want to be here for this."

My parents turn their attention to the wall, where a new painting has just been hung. Its canvas is hidden behind a purple silk sheet. The artist stands nearby, his smock splattered with paint.

"Are we ready?" asks the painter.

Mother and Father reply at the same time. "Ready!"

The artist grabs hold of the sheet and pulls. All of a sudden my jaw drops. I find myself looking back at . . .

Myself.

It's a painting of me. Hanging here in the Hall of Kings, among all my great ancestors. My blue eyes stare confidently out from the canvas. In one hand, I'm grasping a sword. In the other, I seem to be holding a shiny black device.

"Wait, is that . . ." I point an uncertain finger at the painting. "A *Self-Own?*"

My father nods excitedly. "We wanted something that would represent your journey to Urth. And from what you've told us, everyone there has a Self-Own."

"The last time he visited, Mr. Estrada gave us his old one," Mother says. "He said it didn't work anymore because of a dead nattery."

I wrinkle my brow. "You mean *battery?*"

"That's the word!"

"We gave it to the artist," Father explains. "And he incorporated it into your portrait."

Mother looks from one version of me to the other. The boy in the painting and the boy standing beside her. "Don't you like it?"

"I do," I say. "It's just . . . unexpected. This is the Hall of Kings. And I'm, well—not a king."

"Not *yet*," Father points out.

"We know it's rather early," Mother continues. "But after everything you've done for the kingdom—"

"And for us," Father adds.

"The time was right." Mother pats me on the shoulder with a bejeweled hand. "Even if you're not yet a king, you've earned your place in history."

At the bottom of the frame is a gold nameplate. Leaning forward, I peer more closely at the words that have been inscribed into its shiny surface.

PRINCE FREDERICK XIV
DEFENDER OF HELDSTONE,
EXPLORER OF URTH

Emotion wells up inside me. I do my best to look princely and dignified, but I can't pull it off. A huge grin splashes across my face.

"I'm honored. Thank you." I turn from the artist to my parents. "Honestly, I could stand here and stare at myself for hours. But we should probably be going."

"Of course," Mother says. "Mustn't be late for our meeting."

Father is already sweeping in the direction of the doorway. "I can hardly wait."

We hurry down a long corridor, up a spiraling staircase. Servants bow as we pass. Turning a corner, I nearly trip over a big, slobbering pile of fur.

Robbie.

The dog grins up at me, tail wagging. "Hiya, Mr. Prince! Wanna play fetch?"

"I'm afraid I can't at the moment, Robbie," I say. "But if you'd like to join us, there might be fetch where we're going."

Robbie nods eagerly. Drool splatters my shoe. "That sounds awesome!"

And we're off again.

Soon we reach our destination. The Chamber of Wizardry. Back when the Sorceress used this space as her evil workshop, the door was nearly always closed. Locked. But now that this room has a new occupant, the door is wide open. And the Royal Wizardess looks as if she's expecting us.

"Greetings," Desmelde calls out.

Xyler weaves between her ankles. "Just in time."

Mother looks around expectantly. "Has our visitor arrived yet?"

"Not yet." Desmelde waves us through the doorway. "Come inside."

The Chamber of Wizardry is a *much* more inviting place now. Within days of her arrival, Desmelde had her assistants clear away every last remnant of the Sorceress.

Leering gargoyle statues, books of dark spells, all manner of wretched poisons. Now the walls are lined with concoctions intended to *help*, rather than harm. Remedies for the kingdom's most common illnesses, a potion that boosts farmers' crop yields tenfold, water purification serums.

But we didn't come here to inspect Desmelde's inventory. We came for *that*—

The door.

The miniature wooden door.

Leaning down, I grab the handle and give it a sharp tug. Nothing. The door doesn't budge. It never does. Because of course, the door must be opened by someone from the other side. Someone from Urth.

"It appears as though she is running late," the healer says.

"You know how it is for Urthling children." Xyler rolls his eyes. "Always in the middle of a million different activities. School, sports, homework. Not to mention gumpooters—"

"*Computers*," I correct him.

To be honest, I wouldn't mind having some Urth technology right now. If only we could send each other an email or a text. Believe me, we've tried. I borrowed a "tablet" from her world (which looked nothing like the tablets we have in Heldstone). But as soon as it crossed through the miniature doorway, the screen went blank.

CLICK!

The sound comes from the other side of the door. The handle twists and the door opens.

Kara has to hunch as she steps over the threshold. From her world to mine.

She pushes her hair out of her face, surveying our strange group. Me and my parents. A blind wizardess. And two different talking animals.

Just your average trip to Heldstone.

"Hi, everyone." Kara waves. "Who's ready for a burger?"

Kara

It's like Fred and I are enrolled in some kind of inter-dimensional foreign exchange program. Sometimes he visits me. Sometimes I visit him. We hang out in his world—or mine—for a few hours. Then we go back to our lives.

That's been our status for the past month. Sure, it's a hassle to arrange our schedules around these little meet-ups, but what other option do we have? It's not like they have Skype in Heldstone.

But let me back up for a second.

After defeating the Sorceress and bringing Fred's family back to the throne, Dad and I had just one thing on our minds: getting back home. After saying our goodbyes, we charted a quick course back to the Chamber of Wizardry. The miniature wooden door. The portal to Earth.

Except . . . when Dad and I stepped out of the walk-in refrigerator, I had no idea where we were. There was no sign of Legendtopia. Not the cheesy fantasy-themed restaurant where I first went for a field trip *or* the dark castle the Sorceress had transformed it into.

This was another place entirely.

Dad and I emerged from the walk-in fridge, blinking dazedly at our surroundings. We were outside. An early-morning chill clung to the air. The first rays of sunlight had just begun to pierce the darkness.

We were in the middle of a dump. Literally. All around us were huge mounds of trash. Deflated tires, broken electronics, stained mattresses. I pinched my nose, but it didn't do much against the smell. Rot, decay, garbage. It was everywhere.

Welcome back to Earth.

Dad stumbled over a detached car door, his eyes scanning the area. "This looks like the Shady Pines Landfill and Recycling Center. I used to come here all the time."

"Hold up. You're telling me you used to hang out at the *dump?*"

Dad nodded. "It was a great place to find supplies. Old

electronics and scrap metal. I could build all kinds of things with the stuff people throw away."

Throw away. The words sparked an idea. "That's why we're in the middle of a landfill. The walk-in fridge must've been thrown away."

Dad turned to face me. "Why?"

"The explosion in Legendtopia. It destroyed everything. Would've killed me and Fred if it hadn't been for the refrigerator. After that kind of damage, I'm guessing all that was left of Legendtopia was rubble. Whatever they couldn't salvage or resell would have ended up here."

Sure enough, as I inspected my surroundings more closely, I began to notice other artifacts from Legendtopia. The smashed and charred remains of a suit of armor. A stuffed ogre that looked like it had been barbecued. A unicorn's horn, blackened and twisted.

The Sorceress's army, reduced to trash.

"We should be just on the outskirts of Shady Pines. About a half hour from"—Dad's voice cracked. He took a deep breath. "A half hour from *home.*"

Emotion filled Dad's features. He dropped to sit on an old microwave, head resting in his hands. I could only scratch the surface of what he must've been feeling. It felt like I'd been in Heldstone for ages, but it'd actually only been a few days. Dad had been gone a few *years.* Away from his family. Away from the life he'd known on Earth. And now, after all this time, he was back.

Home. At last.

Or: *almost*. We still needed to figure a way out of this dump and back to the house.

Opening my purse, I started to reach for my phone. My hand froze at the sound of muted scuffling inside the inner compartment. The owl. Still flapping. Something else that wanted to find its home.

I no longer needed the magical navigation system. It had served its purpose. And so I opened the compartment. This time, rather than grabbing hold of the necklace like a leash, I allowed the little silver bird to flap freely into the air. It flew a few feet, over a landscape of garbage, and found the person it had been seeking after all this time.

Dad.

He held out his hand, breaking into a smile as the owl perched on his finger.

"Do you remember what you said when you gave it to me?" I asked.

Dad nodded. "If you keep this necklace with you . . ." His eyes sparkled with tears. "It'll bring you closer to me."

"It worked," I said.

Dad traced his thumb across the owl's metallic head and wings. "It certainly did."

"You should keep it. It's just gonna spend all its time trying to book a flight back to you anyway."

Dad gave this some thought. "Maybe you're right. Tell you what—I'll get you a new necklace once we're back home."

And speaking of home . . . I reached back into my purse and grabbed my phone. This time, when I swiped a finger over the screen, the thing lit up. I let out a happy whoop.

"It works!"

I'd never been so excited about technology in my life. I opened my contacts and clicked on "Mom." She answered before the first ring.

"Kara? Kara? Is that you?"

Desperation clung to her voice. It had been days since I disappeared without a trace. Mom must've been devastated. First her husband, now her daughter. All of a sudden, I felt like the worst person in the world.

"Hey, Mom," I said. "It's me."

She burst into sobs. A wave of emotion spilling through the phone. Relief and joy and love.

After several seconds, Mom took a deep breath and spoke in a half whisper. "Are you okay, Kara?"

"I am now." I glance up at Dad. "And I brought someone back with me."

⁓

For most people, the dump wouldn't be the best spot for a family reunion. But for us, all that mattered was being back together again. Mom and my little brother, Neal, pulled up in the car a half hour later. There were a whole lot of group hugs and grateful tears. Then came the ride home. And the questions. Sooooo many awkward questions.

Where have you been all this time?

A magical portal? Inside a *refrigerator*?

What's a *fwarf*?

Dad and I tried to explain, but I could see Mom's and Neal's faces scrunch with bewilderment. Our experiences sounded unbelievably insane and insanely unbelievable. The kind of stuff you'd read about in an old fantasy book or see in a blockbuster movie.

The truth was going to take a while to sink in.

I also had questions of my own. I hadn't seen my mom or brother since the Sorceress transformed our town, unleashing her fantastical foot soldiers into the streets and brainwashing the population of Shady Pines. But the more I prodded at the subject, the more I realized: Mom and Neal had no idea what I was talking about.

"It's kinda weird," Neal said. "A bunch of stuff in town got damaged and destroyed, but nobody knows how it happened. Police tried to check video footage, but guess what?" Neal's eyes widened. "All the security cameras had malfunctioned. All of them. Freaky, huh?"

"Super-freaky," I said. And also super-unsurprising. I'd seen what the Sorceress could do to electronic equipment. It was the same thing she did to people's minds. Infiltrating them like a computer virus. Brainwashing people, causing gadgets to malfunction. And now that her reign of terror was finally over, the town of Shady Pines was left with a case of mass amnesia and a lot of property damage.

The more I questioned Mom and Neal, the clearer it became that the Sorceress's spell had been lifted when she returned to Heldstone. The magical minions, the talking animals, the killer playground equipment . . . all back to what they'd been before.

Ordinary animals and lifeless objects.

On the way home, we drove right past Legendtopia. Or what *used to be* Legendtopia. As the car approached, I jumped forward in my seat, staring out the window.

There was the shopping center. But in the place where

the fake fantasy castle once stood, there was only a crater. A massive dent in the ground. Rubble and dirt and ashes. Nothing more.

So long, Legendtopia.

———

Over the next few weeks, we had to figure out how to be a family again. It wasn't always easy. When Dad left the room, Mom's entire body would tense up. As if she was afraid he'd go missing again as soon as he left her sight. Neal had been six when our father disappeared. Sometimes he'd peer across the dining room table at Dad like a stranger had just joined us for dinner. In some ways, Dad *was* a stranger. So much had happened in our lives over the past years. We had a lot of catching up to do. I looked forward to every second of it.

Other than Mom and Neal, I haven't told anyone else about what really happened. That includes my best friend, Marcy. Although she's starting to get suspicious. On the day I'm supposed to meet with Fred, my phone keeps buzzing with new texts. And they're all from Marcy.

> something's going on w you

> youve been acting really weird lately

> all mysterious and stuff

youre hiding something

And I know what it is!!!

Kara has a boyfriend!!! Kara has a boyfriend!!!

I stare at the screen. With all my secrets and sneaking around lately, I totally understand why she'd jump to that conclusion. But the truth is, I'm not ready to think about the b-word. Not yet, anyway. My otherworldly long-distance friendship with Fred is complicated enough already.

But if there's anyone who deserves to know the truth—about Heldstone, about Prince Fred, about the adventures we shared—it's Marcy. She's not only my best friend. She's also the biggest fantasy fan I know.

Tapping the screen, I text Marcy back.

You're wrong about the boyfriend

But I DO have news

Only if you PROMISE, PROMISE, PROMISE
you can keep a secret

Wanna come over tonight??

I open the back door and jog across the grass. Up ahead, hidden from our neighbors by a tall wooden fence and half shielded by overgrown bamboo plants, is something you wouldn't normally find in a backyard: a char-blackened, heavily dented steel box that my family brought back from the landfill, strapped to the roof of our car.

I open the door of the walk-in refrigerator and climb inside. Making my way across the cramped, dim room, I duck underneath a shelf. Along the way, the walls change from metal to brick. The darkness is pierced by a duo of flaming torches. Between them stands a miniature wooden door.

I twist the handle and push it open.

There's a whole crowd of people (and a couple of animals) waiting for me on the other side.

"Hi, everyone." I wave to the group. "Who's ready for a burger?"

⸺

It's a perfect night for a party.

In one corner of the backyard, my dad's giving barbecue tips to the King of Heldstone. Between them, food simmers on the grill. My brother tosses the Frisbee to Robbie.

"Great catch!" Neal yells to the dog.

"Awesome throw!" the dog yells back.

At the table, Desmelde is adding her own magical topping to the potato salad. Nearby, my mom is showing her phone to the queen and Xyler.

The queen tentatively swipes a finger over the screen. "How utterly marvelous!"

"Do you mind if we watch another cat video?" Xyler asks.

From the porch, Marcy stares at this scene. Her mouth hangs open, showing off a gleaming set of braces.

After pinky-swearing her to secrecy, I told Marcy everything. But now that she's seeing it for herself, I can tell she'll need some time to adjust to the unreal reality on display.

Her gaze shifts slowly across the yard. When she speaks, her voice is full of wonder.

"This. Is. *Epic!*"

I let out a laugh. "I know it's not what you expected, but I figured you—of all people—deserve to know the truth."

Fred stands beside her. The last time they met, we convinced Marcy he was an exchange student from England. She thought he was impressive then. Now she's completely blown away.

"So, you're a prince?" she asks.

Fred nods.

"Like, a *real* prince? Of a *real* kingdom?"

Fred nods again.

"And in your world," Marcy continues, "you have magic and dragons and trolls?"

"Actually, one of our closest friends is a troll!" Fred replies.

"His name's Groo," I add. "I wanted to invite him, but he's too big to fit through the portal."

Marcy blinks. "Your friend . . . is a troll?"

"A vegetarian troll," I say. "With free-range chickens. You'll have to meet him sometime."

A grin forms on Marcy's face. "Okay, that's officially the coolest thing anyone's ever said to me."

___

Grabbing a seat on a bench, I gaze across the yard. The king and queen are laughing with my parents. Neal's trying on Prince Fred's robe, strutting across the yard like royalty. Marcy looks like she couldn't be more excited to share a table with a wizardess and two talking animals.

"I'd say the party is a success." Prince Fred lowers himself onto the bench beside me, his paper plate piled high with food. "Although I'm still getting used to the idea that my *plate* is made of *paper*."

"Right." I roll my eyes. "As if *that's* the weirdest thing about tonight."

He gives me a closer look. "Remember what you said to me back in Heldstone? The night we met Gerta? When we were having a picnic outside the stable?"

I try to recall our conversation. "You'll have to remind me."

"You said maybe someday we could just be typical kids. No evil witch chasing us, no danger hanging over our lives. You know, *normal*."

Fred's voice brings the memory back into my mind. Leaning against the stable wall, gazing up at the seven full moons.

"Well, the Shadow Queen is gone," he says. "The grand duke's soldiers aren't chasing us. And we're here—enjoying dinner with family and friends. Just like typical kids. You got what you wanted."

He's right. I mean, sure, we still have to meet up in a magical refrigerator whenever we want to hang out. But that doesn't seem to matter. Not now. Not on a night like this.

Our situation may not be everyone's definition of "normal." But for me, it's close enough.

Did you read the first LEGENDTOPIA book?

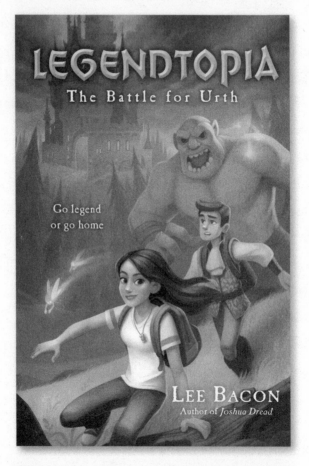

Magic is spreading. A dark kingdom is rising.

And the fate of two worlds rests

in Kara's and Fred's hands.